Bellini and the Sphinx

a novel by

TONY BELLOTTO

Translated from Brazilian Portuguese
by Clifford E. Landers

MYS BELLOTTO

BROOKLYN, NEW YORK, USA
BALLYDEHOB, CO. CORK, IRELAND

Published by Akashic Books
©2019 Tony Bellotto

Published with the support of the Brazilian Ministry of Culture / National Library Foundation.
Obra publicada com o apoio do Ministério da Cultura do Brasil / Fundação Biblioteca Nacional.

 MINISTÉRIO DA CULTURA
Fundação BIBLIOTECA NACIONAL

Paperback ISBN: 978-1-61775-662-7
Library of Congress Control Number: 2018931233

Akashic Books
Brooklyn, New York
Ballydehob, Co. Cork, Ireland
Twitter: @AkashicBooks
Facebook: AkashicBooks
E-mail: info@akashicbooks.com
Website: www.akashicbooks.com

For my father

According to me, it was as foolish to try to read character from the shape of ears as from the position of stars, tea-leaves, or spit in the sand; anybody who started hunting for evidence of insanity in himself would certainly find plenty, because all but stupid minds were jumbled affairs . . .
—Dashiell Hammett

MAY 17

Thursday

1

Before I was awake I could already hear the annoying sound of a telephone ringing insistently. I was floating in an intermediate state between deep sleep and wakefulness and arose to hear my own voice grunting in an attempt (futile) to say hello.

I recognized Rita's high-pitched voice yelling from the other end of the line: "Bellini! Where've you been? Dora wants to see you at two o'clock sharp."

"What time is it?" I asked with a yawn.

"Ten till noon. I've been calling all morning. Where were you?"

"Sleeping," I replied, and she knew that a phone call wasn't always enough to make me open my eyes.

I said goodbye with a "Be there right away," leaped out of bed, took a cold shower, shaved.

I walked down Peixoto Gomide to the August Moon, at the intersection with Alameda Santos, and sat down in one of the sidewalk chairs. Antonio, the waiter, served me my usual salami sandwich with provolone cheese on French bread, cold beer on tap, and a short and bitter espresso, no sugar. "What's up?" he asked.

"Possibly a new case. I don't know yet . . ."

"Adultery?"

"Must be."

The sky was a blue that can only exist in May. I took a taxi to the Itália Building, where Dora Lobo commanded her investigations.

Routine cases of adultery made up the greatest part of our work, which was mostly boring (I dozed off for a few seconds during the ride).

I went into the office on the fourteenth floor. Rita greeted me with her ironic and inevitable "good morning." I caught Lobo in her private office, enjoying two of her favorite habits: smoking an American Tiparillo cigarette and playing Paganini at high volume.

It was a good sign.

2

I had been working for Dora Lobo, *Detective Lobo* as she was known, for a year.

She told me to sit, turned down the volume of the Paganini using the remote control lying on her desk, and after a deep drag put out what was left of the cigarette.

"Yesterday, in the early afternoon, I received a phone call from a man who wanted to meet me in 'absolute confidentiality,' as he repeated several times, 'after eight at night.' He identified himself as 'Dr. Rafidjian, pediatric surgeon.' At eight thirty he showed up, a very tall, thin guy with a long, melancholy face, somewhere between forty-five and fifty, extremely shy. Know who he made me think of?"

"No."

"Don Quixote. Kind of stooped over, he was carrying a doctor's bag and an umbrella. He sat down, resting the bag and the umbrella on his knees, and asked me in an almost inaudible voice, 'Do you guarantee me absolute confidentiality?' I answered, 'Confidentiality is the primordial condition for the exercise of an investigation.'"

Dora and her phrases, I thought, while she opened a drawer and took out a printed sheet of paper and slid it across the desk for me to take a look. It was the contract.

"The man begged: 'I need you to discover the whereabouts of a young woman. A girl barely eighteen named Ana Cíntia Lopes. She was a dancer at the Dervish, a nightclub on Rua Augusta. A little over a month ago she simply disappeared.' Desperate at the girl's sudden vanishing, Don Quixote decided on his own to interrogate employees and customers of the Dervish in search of her whereabouts. The investigation was a dead end; to his surprise, no one there knew an Ana Cíntia Lopes."

3

"How could anyone at the Dervish not know her if you yourself said she worked there as a dancer?"

"I implore you to respect my constraints. Because of my reputation I have always avoided frequenting such places. Speaking frankly, Mrs. Lobo, I've never been inside the Dervish or any other nightclub. Therefore, it was Ana Cíntia herself who told me she worked there as a dancer."

"Then you admit she lied?"

"Maybe . . ."

"Lied when she said her name was Ana Cíntia, or when she claimed she worked at the Dervish?"

"I don't know, and that's why I'm here. To find out."

"Mr. Rafidjian, be more clear! How did you meet Ana Cíntia if you never set foot in the Dervish or any other such establishment?"

"I never went in, but for some time now I've been an uncommitted voyeur . . ."

"What do you mean?"

"I would park my car on the opposite side of the street and study the movement of people in front of the Dervish. Whenever I had some free time between visits with patients, I was there in my car, observing. That was how I noticed a dark-complexioned young woman with brown eyes filled with indescribable sadness. I always saw her. Going in, coming out, or just standing on the sidewalk. I fell in love before she even knew I existed. One day I worked up the courage to ask her to get into my car and go for a drive . . ."

"And then?"

"She accepted."

4

Rafidjian and Ana Cíntia started meeting periodically, at times previously agreed upon by telephone. This went on for six months, more or less. At the beginning of April they set up a meeting as usual in front of the Dervish. Ana Cíntia didn't show up. After that, Don Quixote had no word of her: the girl had disappeared without a trace.

Dora stared at me in silence after recounting the exchange. I looked at her hair, still luxuriant for a woman of sixty. The picture of a successful woman: independent, living alone, subtly ambiguous (single), discreetly egocentric (only child), and absolutely proud of an intelligence as intimidating as a gun pointed at your forehead.

"Obviously, before Rafidjian left, I put him through a series of questions: Where did Ana Cíntia live? Did she have friends? Relatives here in São Paulo or another city? Was she in danger—did she feel threatened? Enemies? Pimps, protectors? Did she use drugs? To each of these the doctor shook his head. Finally, he said: 'I know nothing about her. I do know she's pure, ingenuous, childlike, and why not say it, a bit diabolical . . .' After that odd comment he said good night and that was all."

I shifted my gaze to the Persian carpet spread under the desk and asked, "Is there a photo of the girl?"

"No, just a vague description: brown shoulder-length hair, dark eyes and thick eyebrows, a squarish face, and a slim body with muscular legs. No distinguishing moles, marks, or scars."

Dora got up, went to the cabinet, poured herself a glass of port. She offered me a Scotch, which I didn't refuse. We toasted, drank. She went to the window, looked down at the cars moving along Avenida Ipiranga.

"I guess I should begin by gathering some information over on Rua Augusta," I concluded. "Starting tonight at the Dervish. Keep me informed."

She returned to her desk and consulted her appointment book. "Call Iório, in the Fourth Precinct." She shoved a sheet of paper toward me with a phone number. "He's a friend and knows the area well." She picked up the remote and Paganini came back at full volume. Then she extended her hand and dismissed me by pointing the wineglass in my direction. "Good luck, Bellini."

Bellini. My name is Remo. Remo Bellini. It so happens that I detest that name Remo, and there's a good reason for it. Let me explain: on a certain fifth of June I was expelled from the womb of Livia Bellini along with my twin brother Romulo. The idea of baptizing the newborns with the names of the legendary founders of Rome came from Tulio Bellini, our father.

Tulio, at the time a young criminal lawyer just starting his career, was overflowing with paternal pride at learning he had sired two identical beings, male and primogenitary.

For a short time, however. Unexpectedly, as is its style, fate threw a bomb at Livia and Tulio: Romulo, unable to resist, succumbed to an attack of pneumonia two days after birth.

That's when my problems began.

5

I was forming a mental image of Ana Cíntia Lopes as I stepped into the taxi. "Avenida Paulista, corner of Peixoto Gomide."

On the radio, a baritone with a modulated voice was singing an aria. Opera singers always made me think of my father. I can still hear his voice saying: *If Romulo had survived, I'm certain I wouldn't have to live with so many disappointments.* Of course he blamed me for almost all of them. Or: *If a word to the wise is sufficient, you would need four or five. A pity that most of the time, ten or eleven aren't even enough.* At the same time, phrases like that instilled in me a secret desire to redeem Romulo's absence, fueled an unspoken rivalry between the two of us (as if death, in a terrible mistake, had taken the wrong brother, the one born to fulfill paternal expectations).

I was alone then, unprotected, besieged by a father who attributed to me his disappointments, and by the silent specter of my brother, bearing on my shoulders two ridiculous names that were nothing more than the cold expression of the pedantry of Tulio Bellini: Romulo and Remo.

Gradually I became Remo the Two-in-One.

That sounds strange, even funny, but it faithfully expresses how I felt for much of my childhood, a two-in-one. And it also explains why, from an early

age, whenever I was asked my name I would just reply, "Bellini." By freeing myself of Remo I also freed
myself of Romulo, and was able to live a normal life
with a normal name: just Bellini.

In the old Baronesa de Arary building, where I rented
a kitchenette, I spent the rest of the afternoon listening to Muddy Waters on tape. My neighbor, an
elderly spinster, banged on the wall several times to
complain about the noise, at one point waking me
from a confused dream in which a dog was growling
at me but I didn't feel the slightest fear.

6

At the Dervish I asked a barman with an opaque
gaze if any dancer had disappeared in the last few
weeks. He pointed me toward a guy sitting at a table:
"That's a question for Khalid. Ask him." Khalid was
a solid man, a little past fifty, with abundant hair
and a black mustache.

"Khalid's your boss?" I asked.

"Khalid and his brother Tufik are the managers.
But before you get too excited, be careful. He's a
weird guy."

I went over to the table where the Bedouin (Khalid looked like a Bedouin) was sitting lost in thought,
smoking a Bahian cigar and staring into infinity.

"Mr. Khalid?"

He looked at me gently. "Yes, son?"

"I'm looking for a missing dancer. Her name is Ana Cíntia Lopes."

"Police?"

"No. Lobo Private Investigations."

"Have a seat. Want something to drink?"

"No thank you."

"Ana Cíntia Lopes." He thought for several seconds while blowing cigar smoke in my direction (a Suerdieck, I supposed). "I don't know her."

"Have any of the dancers suddenly disappeared?" I pressed.

Khalid raised his eyebrows in an expression of powerlessness, then bared his teeth in a smile. "They disappear all the time, don't they?" Assuming a complicitous air, as if we were simply two old buddies catching up in a bar, he went on: "They're always making trouble, but like we say around here, they're a necessary evil. Where would the fun be in life without them? You tell me, Mr. Detective, where would the fun be in life without them, huh?"

That "huh" carried unexpected aggressiveness. I felt I should respond, though I had little desire for that kind of conversation.

"Right . . . no fun."

Khalid gave another derisive smile. "The name

doesn't matter, there are so many of them! And deep down they're all alike. Why bother with one of them when deep down they're all alike, huh?"

That "huh" was even more unsettling.

"They're all alike, that's it," I said.

"Ana Cíntia, Ana this, Ana that . . . For every one that vanishes five more show up the next day. Maria Something-or-Other, Maria From-Somewhere, Maria Don't-Know-Who . . . What difference does the name make? Ha ha ha . . . What difference does the name make if what we're looking for in all of them has the same name: pussy!"

7

There was something hysterical in Khalid. He continued his explanation about women: "Take it from me, women are an illusion. And dancers even more so. Don't believe your own eyes, don't believe your own nose, don't believe your own senses. And above all, don't believe your own dick!" Khalid sucked on his cigar lewdly, smoke mixing with the incessant gush of words from his mouth. "Women are like champagne: they seem real but they only exist as long as there's music in the air. I can prove it."

The conversation was becoming too philosophical for my taste. "Sir, I'm only trying to find out if any of the dancers disappeared recently—"

"Forget that nonsense, son. Looking for a dancer
. . . a waste of time! I'm gonna prove to you that
woman are an illusion. Close your eyes."

"What?"

"Close your eyes, detective!" he ordered, pointing his cigar in the direction of the stage where naked dancers gyrated to music.

I closed my eyes. (*Don't contradict a crazy man, he
might be armed*, Dora would say.)

"And now, what do you sense?"

"I hear lousy music and can smell a cigar."

"A cigar? Don't play me for a fool, detective. You
smell pussy. And you know what? They all smell the
same."

"Honestly, Mr. Khalid—"

"Don't get me wrong," he interrupted. "What
I mean is that you couldn't distinguish an Ana . . .
Ana . . ."

"Cíntia," I supplied.

"An Ana Cíntia from a Maria de Fatima by the
smell of their . . . vaginas. Women are all the same.
Keep your eyes closed and try not to breathe for a
moment . . . Do it!"

I closed my eyes again and pinched my nostrils,
asking myself what I was doing there.

"And now, detective, what do you sense?"

"I hear *busic*," I said, with my nostrils still shut.

"You see? Women don't exist. They're an illusion. Like champagne, like music!" He now placed his hand on mine. "Don't cause any trouble in my house, huh? The customers don't like it." He smiled with infinite goodness. "Now, with your permission, Khalid is leaving. Good luck, son."

He got up and vanished into the darkness of the Dervish.

For several minutes I was unable to react. Gradually, the pile-driving reverberation of the strident music brought me out of my lethargy. I observed the mechanical movement of the dancers onstage; one of them smiled lasciviously at me.

If that was an illusion, at least it was an illusion with large, succulent breasts.

8

Her hair was long and black like an odalisque, and her eyes shone like a snake's. (I don't know if a snake's eyes actually shine, but at that moment in my imagination they did).

I remained seated at the table where Khalid had just taught me some of the secrets of female nature. The place smelled musty. I asked the waitress for a beer. For someone who said women were an illusion, he kept a large number of them at his service. She poured the beer from a dark bottle, filling the glass till the foam spilled out. She smiled. I took a slow sip, pointed the glass toward the dancer, and used it to trace an imaginary ellipse, inviting her to the table. She responded with her hands while soundlessly moving her lips, miming the word *later*. And then she went on dancing, looking at me with those lascivious eyes.

After ten minutes, she sat down beside me.

"Something to drink?" I asked.

"Anything."

I ordered more beer.

"What's your name?"

"Fatima, and yours?"

"Bellini."

A few seconds of silence.

"Fatima, I think you can help me."

"I can?" She smiled ambiguously.

"Not the way you're thinking."

"No? Are you sure?"

"Fatima, I'm not sure of anything. Never have been. Don't ask me if I'm sure of a single thing."

"Oh." She frowned, made a wry face, then said, "So tell me, Bellini, how can I help you?"

"I'm looking for a girl named Ana Cíntia Lopes."

"Who?"

Maybe Khalid was right, and Ana Cíntia was just an illusion of Dr. Rafidjian's.

"Ana Cíntia!" I said impatiently. "Or some other name—whatever. But she works here, or used to work here."

"Not by that name. No." With suspicion in her eyes, she asked, "Are you a cop?"

"Do I look like a cop?"

She stared at me intensely and then said: "Yes."

"I look like a cop? Me? Well, you know what you look like?"

Fatima's eyes widened as she awaited the answer.

"A whore."

"But I *am* a whore!"

9

Yes, I have problems with being mistaken for a cop. The provocation of calling her a whore hadn't worked, so I resumed the conversation on a softer note.

"I'm a private detective, Fatima."

"And what's the difference between a private detective and a police detective?"

"The same as between the bathroom in my house and a public urinal."

"But I've never seen the bathroom in your house," she said.

"Okay, Fatima, I get the feeling you don't want to help me."

"No, I'm just kidding . . . I understood what you meant. You feel you're morally better than a cop, is that it?"

"That's it."

"Then tell me what this Ana Cíntia is like."

I took some time to formulate the reply: "I don't know."

"That makes it hard."

A momentary silence fell between us.

It was true: I didn't know who I was looking for or even why.

I stared at Fatima and sensed an attraction beginning to manifest itself in my pants. Despite the erotic nature of the situation, I also felt the need to urinate, so I excused myself to the bathroom. I waited for my hard-on to subside, and as I pissed I noted that the urinal reminded me of a baptismal font. The vision of that baptismal font defiled by urine brought back memories hidden in corners of my mind. For example, the murmurs of my mother at Sunday Mass, repeating to the point of exhaustion a monotonous phrase that to me was extremely disturbing and enigmatic: "Lamb of God, who takes away the sins of the world, have mercy on us."

And the voice of my father when I told him of my decision to leave his law practice: "You're going to abandon a noble and promising profession as a lawyer to get involved with people of questionable character in places where not even minimum morality is respected? That's absurd."

Or the words of my ex-wife in the note announcing her departure, left among the rumpled sheets on our bed: *I married a man of ideals and principles, not a boy who refuses to grow up and insists on believing in fantasies and detective stories.*

The cold water from the faucet drove away the ghosts and brought me back to the bathroom at the Dervish. I returned to the table expecting to find Fatima gone, but she was still there, with her large breasts and her ophidian eyes. I sat down, pulled my chair over to hers, and decided to be more objective: "If you help me solve this case, Fatima, I'll owe you one."

10

I knew that in the night world, a word of honor is worth more than a signed and sealed contract. And I wasn't mistaken.

Fatima assured me that she had frequented the circuit of nightclubs on Rua Augusta for over three years. Despite having met numerous Ana Marias, Ana Lúcias, Ana Teresas, and various other Anas, she swore she had never heard of any Ana Cíntia. I asked her to recall all the dancers who had left the circuit in recent months. Another flurry of women's names swarmed around me. Even a few transvestites were mentioned, and I didn't rule out the possibility of Ana Cíntia being a man, because as Khalid would say, women are an illusion. At the end of the conversation, however, only two names jibed with "brown shoulder-length hair, dark eyes and thick eyebrows, a squarish face, and a slim body with muscular legs," as the mysterious Rafidjian would describe her. Those were the dancers Camila and Dinéia.

Dinéia had gotten pregnant and, as she didn't want an abortion, had gone to her mother's in the interior of the country.

"Where in the interior?" I asked.

"I don't know, some interior in this Brazil of ours."

Great, I thought, *only a few million square kilometers to search.*

Camila had also disappeared, but Fatima didn't know why.

"Camila is real crazy, always disappearing and coming back more unhinged than ever."

"What do you mean, by *crazy*?"

"Crazy from coke, weed, pills, needles, crack. Whatever there is."

"And where'd she disappear to?"

"She was in rehab somewhere or other . . . in a hospital or an asylum, beats me."

At that moment I looked at my watch: 2:40 a.m.

I remembered that earlier in the afternoon, I had wasted some time trying to reach that Iório guy, the cop from the Fourth Precinct, by phone. I located him at home, where he was still sleeping at five p.m. His wife told me: "Iório traded night for day a long time ago."

"It's urgent."

"But who wants to talk to him?" she asked with a slight Italian accent.

"Bellini, Dora Lobo's assistant."

"Detective Lobo? One moment."

After some minutes Iório greeted me in a hoarse and ill-humored voice. I quickly explained the situation and we agreed to meet at three in the morning at the Bisteca d'Ouro, a bar on Rua da Consolação.

I hurriedly left the Dervish with Fatima in tow, taking her by the Hotel Memphis on Rua Frei Caneca. I gave her some money to make up for the hours of work she had missed.

"Call me if you remember anything."

"Give me your number."

I wrote my home and office numbers on her palm, as they were no blank pages left in my note-pad. Before she got out of the cab—I don't know who initiated it—we kissed. An intense kiss, wet, nervous, inevitable. Her large breasts had bothered me all night. I fondled them over her blouse. They seemed hard to the eye, but when I touched them I found they were soft. The nipples hardened like stone and stuck out in high relief under the smooth dark fabric of her blouse.

Fatima disentangled herself and got out of the car, laughing. "You're going to be late for your appointment," she said, closing the taxi door.

As she entered the hotel, I called out: "Do you know a weird doctor who hangs out in his car, observing everything in front of the Dervish?"

"A doctor? No, the only people watching that place are the police, from time to time."

I arrived at the Bisteca d'Ouro just before three o'clock. Some parked police vehicles broadcasted metallic voices interspersed with static out onto the sidewalk.

11

In the year I worked as an assistant lawyer to my father, I was treated more like an intern than a fullfledged attorney. That meant endless hours sitting idly at his desk. I had the illusion that I would become a great criminal lawyer just by being there, sitting where Tulio Bellini was accustomed to sitting. That gave me the feeling that things were under control. I would phone my wife every half hour to say, "I love you," and I thought our marriage would last forever. Sometimes I would ask the secretary, Dona Helga, for coffee, light up one of the Havanas (Montecristo Number 2) that rested in a light-colored box on the desk, and examine the books on the shelves. Generally, titles on criminal justice didn't strike me as particularly interesting, but there were other volumes that attracted me. Pierre Grimal's *Dictionary of Classical Mythology* was one. One day I pulled it from the bookcase and flipped the pages at random, not focusing on anything until I got to the letter R. Instinctively, I looked for the entry *Remo*.

> REMO (*Remus*). *In the legend of the founding of Rome, Remo is the twin brother of Romulo. According to one explanation, obviously of late origin, he had been given the name of Remo because he was "slow" in everything. Which would explain why he was supplanted by Romulo. Remo, in the legend, is depicted as the unfortunate "double" of his brother.*

It's true that the name Remo was never totally suppressed from my life, but with one or two exceptions I succeeded in being called Bellini throughout kindergarten, elementary, middle, and high school. And I continued as Bellini in law school.

This gave me a feeling of fulfillment, almost like an anesthetic, and kept those two strange and menacing twins suckled by a she-wolf away from my day-to-day endeavors.

After graduation I became Dr. Bellini, which was short-lived because I never got used to being called doctor.

I survived as Bellini (and I am in fact a survivor), but I never freed myself from Romulo's threatening ghost hovering over my head, reminding me of what I should have been but never was.

12

The Bisteca d'Ouro was a police hangout, and one of the few good things I inherited from Tulio Bellini was a total aversion to cops.

I didn't know Iório but imagined him to be a typical policeman and therefore hard to spot among the cops infesting the Bisteca at that hour of the night, since in general they're all very similar. But something set him apart. Maybe the white stubble, maybe the look of someone who enjoyed taking care of small birds.

As soon as I entered, he welcomed me with open arms, a gesture that I must admit was unusually warm for a policeman. I was a bit suspicious. With cops, as Dora said, *It's best to be on your guard.*

Iório spoke: "Ah, so you're Lobo's new assistant? But she's no wolf, she's a fox."

And there were guffaws, including from other cops, all of them old, almost decrepit, as if they were there for some event in a police retirement home.

"This here is the old guard of the São Paulo police."

Maybe policemen became nicer as they aged.

He introduced me to some of his colleagues, after leading me to a table in the left corner of the room. He asked the waiter for cold beer and a small fillet "to get started." He asked me: "How do you feel about a few slices of French bread to dip in the meat sauce?"

We drank beer and ate slices of bread with fillet garnished with chopped onion, while I related the story and all its details.

After listening to my narrative, Iório didn't say anything. He merely extended his left arm and opened his hand in my direction. With his right hand he summoned a guy who was sitting next to the counter, a skinny kid with a silver ring hanging from his left ear. He wore his hair long despite a devastating receding hairline that gave him a very high forehead. His name was Stone.

Stone couldn't be older then twenty-two and had an arrogant bearing that attempted to disguise his insecurity and fragility. At first I thought he was a young policeman, an investigator or something like that. But Iório's aggressive and ill-humored attitude toward him proved I was wrong. He was an informer.

Iório suddenly changed from a friendly old man into an implacable torturer.

"Stone, you shitty two-bit trafficker. If you don't want to spend some time in the Graybar Hotel, you better do what my friend here wants, understand?"

Stone, surely schooled in police decorum, acquiesced humbly. Iório stood up, kissed my cheek, and left without another word.

Stone and I sat there.

13

We studied each other like two adversaries in a boxing ring. I imagined that Stone only functioned if you turned the screws, as the police jargon put it, but I wasn't a cop and needed to take advantage of this fact. I tried playing the "understanding" card and explained I didn't have the slightest intention of getting him in bad with Iório, and all that crap you say when you want to give the impression you're on the crook's side.

"Get on with it, dude," he said. "I'm in a hurry."

I don't know why, but that statement reminded me of the first time I went to a brothel. It was a yellow house on Alameda Glete, in the downtown area. I was thirteen, a virgin, and went there in the company of an older cousin who knew the place. It was a hot December midafternoon. When I found myself alone with a blond prostitute in a dark, stuffy room, I tried to appear sensitive and friendly. I thought that by showing myself to be different from other customers I could receive attention a little less "professional." But she didn't go for it and instead said: "Stop talking and stick it in, you've only got twenty minutes." And she didn't take off her shirt, just her panties, because "looking at my tits costs extra." I couldn't get an erection, despite all the desperate attempts that used up my allotted twenty minutes.

14

I looked at Stone, who was impatiently awaiting some word.

"Do you know Ana Cíntia Lopes?" I finally asked.

"No."

"What about some dancer at the Dervish who might have disappeared in the last month?"

"A few."

"Then give me their names, physical descriptions, and anything else you know about each of them." I was making every effort to appear serious and professional, like in a real police investigation.

"Well, let's see." He thought for a moment. "There's Dinéia."

"Dinéia?"

"You know Dinéia?"

"Only by name. What's she like?"

"Short dark hair. Slim but with big tits, like in *Playboy*, you know what I mean?"

I nodded.

He continued: "Seems she got pregnant and went home to her family in Paraná."

"What city in Paraná?"

"I don't know, brother, I don't know her all that well. I did some shows with Dinéia at the club. Nice girl."

"Slowly," I said. "I'm taking notes." And I tried to find blank space in my appointment book. "Who else?"

"Simone. She went to Japan with a samba show. She's what you call a monumental mulatta, ya know? She must have latched onto some sucker with little eyes and a big wallet." Stone pulled the corners of his eyes with his fingers in a grotesque imitation.

"Not funny," I said, losing my patience with the idiot.

"All right, you're the boss. Let's see, who else? Yvonne, that cow. Yvonne gave me gonorrhea. You ever had gonorrhea?"

"Me? No."

"Then there's Alessandra. She's cross-eyed. Is the woman you're looking for cross-eyed?"

"No."

"Ruth got her face slashed with a razor. She mouthed off at her pimp. Did you know that *cafiola* in English is pimp?"

"No."

"Well, does the woman you're looking for have a scar on her cheek?"

"No."

"Does she have a tattoo? I know a tramp, Silvia, who's got tattoos on her neck, tits, and—"

"Enough! I'll ask the questions."

My bark attracted Iório's attention, and he approached our table, directing a furious look at Stone. "Any problems here, Bellini?"

"Everything's under control."

Iório walked away, suspicious, and I saw apprehension on Stone's face. I used the opportunity to move the conversation to more objective matters, resuming the position of inquisitor.

"What about Camila? Do you know a Camila?"

"Sure. She used to do a fabulous show with a gringo, a guy named Miguel or Manuel, I don't remember. Been a long time since I last saw Camila."

"What's she like?"

"Fucking beautiful. Slim, a real piece, luscious."

"You know where she is?"

"Probably in Santos. She's from there. Back when she did the show with the gringo, they said she wasn't doing too good, always tired and sick. Camila ain't an easy person. Crazy, a total junkie. I used to supply her with coke. And amphetamines. She can't do without them, she's tough."

"Where would I find her in Santos?"

"Beats me. I think she was gonna try to find work there. Light stuff, ya know how it is."

"No, how is it?"

"She says she wants to get clean, but I don't believe her." He twirled the ring hanging from his ear. "I got a hunch."

"And what might that be?" Outside, the day was brightening.

"Well, I bet she headed straight to the docks. There's a shitload of dives around there. Real cheap drugs and the money comes easy. There's lots of sailors, they pay in dollars, ya know."

"What else?"

"That's all, the end." He looked at me with disdain. "We done here?"

The guy's arrogance was unbearable. I asked: "Do you know a Dr. Rafidjian, a weird guy who sits in his car and watches people going into the Dervish?"

"No."

Stone left and I noticed he limped a little, dragging his right leg. This only reinforced my impression of a shattered character. I ordered a beer and noticed that Iório had also split.

I checked my watch: 6:30. Morning was making itself known through its customary noises: buses and cars in motion, bakeries opening, and news broadcasts crackling from radios.

I would have two hours to write my first report and phone it over to Dora in time to surprise her at the end of her daily aikido exercises.

I asked for the check and strong coffee without sugar. Then I walked out into the cool breeze of morning.

Friday

1

called Dora at eight fifteen. After narrating the events, the reply I got was: "What do you make of it all?"

Me: pale, black rings around my eyes, tired, famished. "I don't know, Dora. You're the one who's got to make something of it. I just gather information."

"Know what I think? I think Khalid is a ridiculous, disagreeable male chauvinist and that his theory about women, besides being extremely vulgar, is the biggest load of crap I've heard in a long time!"

After a brief, awkward silence, during which I lacked the inclination or the rationale to defend Khalid and his theory, she added: "We're on the right track, we just need to find Dinéia and Camila, that's all."

"That's all?"

"Yeah. I want to better analyze certain aspects of your report, so leave it with your doorman. Rita will take care of sending the office boy to collect it. As for you . . ." she paused, "get some sleep and wait for instructions."

We hung up. The old lady was worried, I could tell by her tone. Something about the story didn't fit, but I was tired enough not to let that bother me.

2

I felt like I had barely lain down and closed my eyes when the phone rang. By my watch it was 2:35, which meant I had been asleep at least five hours. I answered.

"Bellini, did I wake you up?"

"No. I mean, yes . . . Who's calling?"

"It's Fatima. I found out where Dinéia is."

"Don't tell me it's Paraná." The last syllable, the *ná*, was pronounced in the form of a yawn.

"How did you know that?" she asked.

"Love, remember that conversation we had about the difference between a private investigator and a police detective? Efficiency is one of the elements of that difference."

"Cool, Bellini. Then you don't need me anymore?"

"I do need you. I know she's in Paraná, but I don't know which city."

"Ah, so you're not that efficient after all, huh?"

Although I couldn't see her, I could feel her eyes flashing at the other end of the line.

"We do what we can," I said. "So what city is she in?"

"Cornélio Procópio. That's where she's from. They told me she was gonna stay at her mother's until the baby is born."

"Well done. When you get tired of life as a dancer, you can try your hand as a detective."

"A female detective?"

"Why not? I know another one."

"Cool, man." A short silence. "Look, I loved the kiss yesterday."

I almost asked, *What kiss?* But instead I said, "Yeah."

"Let's go out one of these days?"

"Call me."

As I dialed Dora I thought how easily a man can lose his head and do something stupid when he drinks a little and sees two large, firm breasts staring him in the face.

3

Lobo was curt: "Go to Santos immediately and don't come back without the address and photos of that Camila."

She reminded me that she'd be expecting daily reports by phone, as was customary. She would then study them on paper upon my return.

I asked about her uneasy tone when we had spoken that morning.

She answered, "It was nothing, I must be getting old and crabby, that's all."

"And what about Dinéia?"

"Leave her to me."

Dora no longer had the patience to leave the office, where she smoked her Tiparillos and listened to Paganini while she pondered her cases. So when she said, *Leave her to me*, I assumed that, as she always did when she needed additional investigative help, she would hire a student or an inexperienced detective (what she dubbed an "intern") and send him to Cornélio Procópio in search of Dinéia.

I gathered my camera, notebook, pen, pocketknife, my 9mm Beretta automatic with silencer—a present from Dora for any eventuality (which I had never used)—and my inseparable companion and friend for all hours, Jack Daniel's. I also grabbed the Walkman and several blues tapes and went down the stairs at the Baronesa de Arary. I was hungry. I stopped at the August Moon for the usual cheese-and-salami sandwich, cold beer, and espresso.

Antonio asked, "Traveling?"

"A quick trip, I'll be back next week."

"Still adultery?"

"In a manner of speaking, yes."

I stood up, grabbed my suitcase, and walked toward Avenida Paulista.

4

I got to Santos at nightfall.

It was stuffy. I found a place on Gonzaga Beach, near Avenida Dona Ana Costa. The receptionist resembled an aged boxer, with a broken nose and flaccid muscles. The room was small and claustrophobic with dirty wallpaper and stained carpets. I left the suitcase there and went back down to the ground floor, where I had a beer in the bar near the reception area. It was crowded—entire families, including dogs, occupying rooms the same size as mine. Incredible what some people do for a weekend at the beach.

I took advantage of a moment of calm and went up to the old boxer.

"Good evening, my name is Bellini." I extended my hand.

"Good evening. Domingos Estrada de Sintra, at your service." He shook my hand firmly. "But you can call me Sintra." I noticed his Portuguese accent, which was in keeping with his name. "You're here for work, aren't you, friend?" he asked.

"Yes, but it's not going to take me very long and," I winked, "while I'm on vacation I'd like to have some fun."

"Ah, I understand." He offered a complicitous smile. "I can arrange some addresses for my friend."

"Will you join me for a beer?" I asked.

"Of course, of course."

Sintra gestured to the barman to bring a bottle to the reception counter. A couple came in—a cadaverous old man and a young woman with perky breasts. She was carrying their luggage, two large suitcases. While Sintra busied himself with them, I stepped out the door and looked around on the sidewalk. A warm night, lots of people in the streets. A bead of sweat ran down my forehead.

I glanced inside. Sintra was again by himself. He called me back, pointing to the bottle of beer. We toasted, clinking glasses. The barman brought a white porcelain plate full of lupine beans to go with the beer. Sintra scooped them into his hand and said, with his mouth full: "Mr. Bellini, I have a better idea."

"About what?" I asked.

"About getting to know the hot places in town, yes?" After a brief pause to swallow the beans, he continued: "My son-in-law drives a taxi. If I phone him and say there's a customer here who wants to see the nightlife in Santos, he'll come right over."

"This very moment?"

"Yes, this very moment!"

Sintra smiled and clicked his tongue against his dentures, nearly pushing them out of his mouth. We drank a bit more and he called his son-in-law Duilio, setting up an appointment for ten thirty.

I still had two hours and would use the time to take a shower, shave, and watch some TV with the sound off, just thinking about life. About *my* life, that is.

5

Before going back up to the room, slightly tipsy, I asked Sintra, "Did you ever box?"

"No. I used to lift weights, but that was a long time ago. Do you ask because of my broken nose?"

I said yes.

"It wasn't fists that broke it." He took a swallow of beer, rinsing his teeth. "Years ago, I was a shot-putter on the track-and-field team of the glorious Portuguesa Santista. During a training session at the Ulrico Mursa Stadium, I was preparing for the first throw of the day. Legs bent, the shot supported on my right shoulder, I began spinning my body, mentally focused, my eyes closed, joined to the shot by the desire to see it fly a great distance, then . . . *bang!* Everything suddenly went black. I fainted. The iron ball fell right onto my nose. The bone shattered, it was terrible." Sintra spit some bean shells into his left hand. "After that, I never threw even a small weight. But lots of years have gone by, and now I'm old. How old is my friend Bellini?"

"Thirty-two, almost thirty-three."

"Well, you still have time to enjoy youth." He raised the glass of beer in my direction. "To youth! To youth in all its doubts and extravagance! The great treasure, the only treasure. Youth!"

Sintra smiled (with tears in his eyes) and his dentures again threatened to jump out of his mouth. I acknowledged the toast with a "Viva!" and returned to my room.

6

Only much later, deep into the night, did I find the lead that would take me to Camila.

Stone, the snitch, was right. I found the lead at the docks, an area frequented by sailors and where drugs were indeed "real cheap."

As a broader investigation strategy I opted to first make a quick sweep of nightclubs, brothels, and other hubs of prostitution in the center of town and near the beaches. I left the dock area for last, in order to afford it a more careful scrutiny. But before arriving there, it would be of interest to learn what took place in the taxi of Sintra's son-in-law Duilio.

He was between thirty-five and forty. Completely

bald, he had a sparse mustache that barely covered his upper lip. The bluish tattoo of an anchor on his left forearm imparted to him the air of a sailor. His battered and wrinkled skin suggested long periods of exposure to the sun. He had a few fetishes hanging from the rearview mirror of the taxi, such as red ribbons of Our Lady of Bonfim and colorful Umbanda beads. Laconic, Duilio limited himself to speaking only when directly addressed.

Around two in the morning, we were driving down Avenida Beira-Mar toward the docks after three hours of futile work. Perceiving the weariness I externalized through a prolonged yawn, he asked point-blank: "Sleepy, boss?"

"A little," I answered.

"If you want, I got something that'll get rid of it."

No great effort of deduction was needed to understand he was referring to cocaine. Although Sherlock Holmes made judicious and productive use of the drug, when I took it, during the last year of my marriage, I didn't have a very happy relationship with it. Of course, it's true that in that fateful year I didn't have a happy relationship with anything. Just the opposite, it was the year my life fell apart. My marriage ended, along with my career as a lawyer, and to this day I don't know what role coke played in that, if any. What I do know is that it was my sole faithful companion while Tulio Bellini and my ex-wife gradually transformed into distant, frightening ghosts.

Even though it was loyal, cocaine never freed me from anguish and depression, and I believe this was the reason I gave it up when I started working with Dora Lobo. (When I met Lobo, a whole new life began for me.) That's why, despite being a bit disturbed, I tried to change the subject by pretending I didn't understand Duilio's insinuation.

"I don't need anything, thanks."

He was insistent: "If you want a little boost, all you gotta do is ask."

"You got any here?"

He nodded.

This changed the course of events. The presence of coke right there, so close, threw me into the seductive claws of temptation. I recalled Freud, to me the foremost detective of all time. He was also a user of cocaine. What great cases must he have solved with its assistance? Like in an animated cartoon, I imagined my head flanked by two small figures—an angel and a devil. The devil was saying, *Sigmund Freud, Sherlock Holmes, Sigmund Freud, Sherlock Holmes . . .* And the angel, *Dora Lobo, Tulio Bellini, Dora Lobo, Tulio Bellini . . .*

"So then, is it a go?" The sailor's voice scared

away angels and devils. But since I had to decide, I opted for the more seductive choice, obviously that of the devil, whispering those two brilliant and charismatic names: "Sigmund Freud, Sherlock Holmes . . ." Then I returned to Duilio: "Okay, but just one line."

He took from his shirt pocket a small vial made especially for the consumption of coke. Its lid unscrewed into a kind of miniature spoon, approximately the size of one nostril. We snorted easily, with the car still in motion, after which we became talkative and more at ease with each other.

7

Whenever I used to do coke, my first sensation was the wish to freeze that state of chemical happiness so it would last forever. Afterward, I would get anxious and a bit suspicious. And it was in that condition, anxious and suspicious, that I was suddenly attacked by one of my old ghosts.

It was the ghost of my ex-wife, and I knew why I was remembering her.

In the last year of our marriage, as if to confirm that it had all been a mistake, my ex-wife, displeased with my professional indecision and my fantasies (which she termed "adolescent"), began periodically disappearing from our house.

At first, under the pretext of going out for drinks with female friends, she would return home in the late hours. Day by day, she would arrive a little later. Then she began to disappear all night, returning after daybreak. Finally, shortly before leaving me for good, she would vanish for two or three consecutive days.

At the time, needless to say, I was confused. Things weren't going very well at the law office, where my father was always demanding a different attitude than the one I was assuming, and maybe that was why I started using cocaine. I never got hooked, not even close. But many times I went out looking for my wife, roaming randomly about the city, nosing around our regular bars, sometimes heading to the bathrooms to snort another line of coke. That was how I stayed awake for entire nights in that useless search; I never found her.

If that didn't help me save the marriage, at least it gave me the basic know-how to later exercise the profession of detective.

The truth is, it was impossible for me *not* to remember my ex-wife (with all the pain it brought) as long as I was doing coke and looking for Camila, a woman, like her, who deep down I didn't know.

8

It was nearly three in the morning when we arrived

at the docks, an area infested with small dives, night-clubs, brothels, and every kind of vice to be found in a city with the largest port in the nation.

Colored lights blinked in different rhythms and the salty smell of the maritime breeze mixed with the odor of stale urine.

I told Duilio to wait for me at a relatively well-lit corner across from a bar, while I explored cobble-stone alleyways. They formed strange geometric patterns, like a labyrinth. Besides the typical characters, to whom I was already accustomed—the hookers, pimps, and drug dealers—the labyrinth introduced many sailors, who despite the various races and nationalities here seemed to be part of a species distinct from us inhabitants of terra firma. To them, the place was merely a port where they were temporarily anchored in search of drugs, booze, and sex.

I spotted a small, poorly lit bar where a group of Chinese sailors were futilely trying to communicate with a biracial transvestite with blond hair.

For the first time, I glimpsed a way out of that labyrinth.

Initially, it seemed like another fruitless effort. I squeezed between the sailors and leaned on the cracked marble of the bar. I mechanically repeated the question I had asked dozens of times.

"Do you know a girl named Camila who showed

up in the last few weeks from São Paulo, eighteen, brown shoulder-length hair, dark eyes and thick eyebrows, squarish face, and a slim body with muscular legs?"

The Portuguese man behind the bar, fat, bald, and unshaven, looked at me, startled. "Talk with Dona Luisa, she's back there in the nightclub."

What he called a nightclub was a darkened room linked to the bar by a passageway the width of a door, hung with colored strips of plastic. Inside, a dim purple light cast its meager illumination on a few couples dancing to the sound of a screechy-voiced singer at full volume. In one corner of the windowless room, sitting beside a record player, a fat old woman with red hair seemed to oversee the setting, controlling what went on around her. I deduced it must be Dona Luisa. I announced myself.

We returned to the relative quiet of the bar so we could talk.

As soon as we reached the counter, the fat Portuguese man immediately said, "Luisa, this fella is looking for that girl, Camila."

Luisa scrutinized me from head to toe. "What do you want with Camila?"

"To find her."

"Why?"

"I'm a client of hers, I come from São Paulo . . . You know how it is, I miss her."

Luisa smiled, a mixture of connivance and suspicion. "I don't know where she lives, but I think I know where she works." She ordered a cognac from the barman, then continued: "The girl looked me up some time back, she wanted a job. But Camila is pretty, a young woman, refined, you know what she's like . . . It wouldn't work for her here . . . I admit I felt sorry for her, she seemed disoriented, without direction, like she'd been dumped by her boyfriend. I decided to help her." She downed a gulp of the cognac. "I just remembered the casino. Do you know the casino?"

"As far as I know, they're outlawed across the country," I replied.

"This is a clandestine club that's open weekends in Cubatão. A very refined place, for high-society people from São Paulo. I think she got a contract there."

"What's the address?" I asked, growing excited.

"Are you the boyfriend who dumped her?"

"No. I'm kind of a . . . carrier pigeon."

The pair found this amusing. Luisa rummaged through a drawer, handed me a piece of paper with the address of the casino, and I dashed for the door, opening a path among the smoke and sailors.

The fat man called after me: "Tonight you won't find anything there. The deal with the police is that it closes down before morning."

I checked my watch: 4:15. By the time I could get to Cubatão it would be daylight. I smacked my fist into my palm. "Shit!"

The two started laughing. The transvestite as well. The drunken Chinese sailors weren't understanding a thing. Neither was I.

As I walked away, I distinguished the voice of Luisa amid all the noise: "Take it easy, love. Tomorrow night at eight o'clock the casino will be back in operation."

On the way back to the hotel, I asked Duilio if he knew the way to the Cubatão casino. His jaws were a bit clenched from the coke.

"Of course."

When we arrived, I said, "Get some rest. Tonight we're going to try our luck at roulette."

He placed his hand over the pocket where he kept the vial of coke, patted it, and smiled as if to say, *There's more where that came from.*

9

In the hotel room, my first impulse was to immediately call Dora; finally, a real, palpable lead. But five a.m. wasn't a convenient hour. So I used the time to work on the written report. Dora was demanding with such write-ups, and grammatical and spelling errors were practically unforgivable. She was a lot like a high school principal. I sometimes wondered if by trading Tulio Bellini's office for Dora Lobo's I had gone from the frying pan into the fire. What basically differentiated Dora Lobo from Tulio Bellini was gender. Tulio was male and Dora, however ambiguous, had a moist cleft between her legs, I was sure of it, though I had never seen her nude.

And perhaps that explained everything.

The circle was narrowing.

At that moment I felt close to finally laying eyes on Camila. It was impossible not to think about Khalid's theory, while in my mind a mysterious dancer named Ana Cíntia split into two others, the ethereal Camila and Dinéia, one of them pregnant and the other dancing in a casino. What would the next surprise be?

I revised the report, and before calling Dora, since I had time to spare, I went down to the breakfast area. In spite of the cocaine, I was really hungry.

I devoured several ham-and-cheese sandwiches, a few bowls of fruit salad, and a couple of steaming cups of coffee with cream. Then I went back to the room and, not even caring if I was interrupting her sacred morning aikido exercises, I phoned Lobo.

"Dora, sorry about calling so early, but I have good news."

"No problem. I was already awake, Beatriz just called."

"Who is Beatriz?" I asked.

"Beatriz is the intern I hired and sent to Cornélio Procópio to look for Dinéia."

"And what did she say?" I tried, but failed, to hide the trace of envy in my voice.

"She said she found Dinéia and even took photos of her. She did more than that—she managed to talk with her, posing as a social worker." Dora was enthused, seemingly proud of this female intern.

"She did all that in one day?"

"What do you think? Beatriz is an excellent young woman. A law student, intelligent and sharp-witted, not to mention charming. You should meet her."

"Meet her and take classes with her—is that what you mean?"

"What's this? You've suddenly become a jealous little boy?"

"And what else did this Beatriz discover about Dinéia?" I asked, hoping she would change the subject.

"You have to stop being so insecure, Bellini. A

man past thirty, a successful and well-paid private investigator, resenting a university student? Don't be like that."

"Don't bust my chops, I don't need your advice. Besides, I don't consider myself all that well paid. Out with it: what did she discover about Dinéia?"

"Show some respect, young man!"

I realized that she was testing me. I asked: "Are you trying to jerk my chain on purpose? Is this a tactic?"

"Exactly. I like to test the sangfroid of my assistants. You're very hotheaded these days. Like I've said before: you need to find a girlfriend."

"A girlfriend, a girlfriend! Wonderful!" I said. "Since we're on the topic, why don't we talk about your sex life a little?"

It was a low blow.

She remained silent for several seconds. "Bellini, dear, certain matters shouldn't be discussed like that, in jest. In any case, not on the telephone. How about we concentrate on Dinéia? Beatriz discovered that her full name is Dinéia Duarte Isidoro and that she actually is pregnant, but it's a precarious pregnancy and she has to rest. She's at her mother's; it's a small house with five siblings, all younger than her. The father is deceased. Beatriz took several photos of Dinéia and the family, claiming they were research for the municipal Department of Social Services. She'll be back today with the prints. There's a good chance Dinéia is our mysterious Dr. Rafidjian's vanished dancer."

"How about that doctor?" I scratched my head. "Weird guy."

"I spent yesterday afternoon on the phone doing some research. Don Quixote really is a pediatric surgeon, one of some renown even. Samuel Rafidjian Jr., forty-eight, married for twenty years to Sofia Aranson Rafidjian, who holds a degree in psychology but doesn't exercise the profession. Apparently a tranquil marriage. Three children: Samuel III, eighteen, who is preparing to follow in his father's footsteps; Silvia, fifteen, and Sergio, ten, are enrolled in a traditional school. They live in a spacious apartment in Higienópolis, with no financial worries. In short, a successful citizen by our society's standards." After a pause to catch her breath, she asked, "And at your end, what have you found out?"

I read her my report. I saw it was well written and felt proud, knowing that Dora Lobo appreciated good detective narratives. Obviously, the report wisely omitted the passages with cocaine, which I could still feel in my bloodstream and was doubtless responsible for my sudden literary inspiration.

Dora said: "It doesn't make sense for you to be

jealous of Beatriz, a pampered twenty-three-year-old who applied for this assignment because she wants to pay her own way to Europe during the July break. Besides which, you're becoming unbeatable in your reports. Your description of the dock area is excellent. I even detect a touch of Simenon." Then, more to character, she added, "Find that Camila right away."

We hung up.

I dragged myself to the bed and listened to John Lee Hooker on the Walkman. Now, in addition to Ana Cíntia, Dinéia, and Camila, I had another woman to worry about: Beatriz.

Women are an illusion, women are an illusion, women are an illusion.

I woke up with Khalid Tureg's phrase reverberating in my brain, which thanks to the cocaine was as alert as if a typhoon were bearing down on it.

MAY 19

Saturday

1

I spent most of the day in a light and anxious sleep. In my semiconscious state, I was assailed by the memory of a passage from the *Remo* entry in the *Dictionary of Classical Mythology*, which I used to read during idle hours in Tulio Bellini's office:

REMO (Remus). *Romulus and Remus agree in principle: they wish to found their city in the place where they were saved, i.e., the site of the future Rome. But the exact location is not yet in their minds, and they decide (on the advice of Numitor) to consult the auguries to reach a verdict. To this end, Romulus installs himself on the Palatine and Remus on the Aventine. The city will be built at the spot where the auguries are propitious. Remus saw six vultures while Romulus saw twelve. The heavens having thus decided in favor of the Palatine (and, as a consequence, of Romulus), Romulus*

begins laying out the limits of his city. Its first demar-
cation is a trench dug by a plow pulled by two oxen.
Remus, profoundly disappointed at not having been fa-
vored by the heavens, mocks this easily overcome pro-
tection and leaps into the interior of the perimeter that
his brother has just consecrated. Romulo, vexed at the
sacrilege, unsheathes his sword and slays Remus.

Remembering these words made me think of
omens. Why did Romulus think the favorable omen
was his?

Aren't vultures foreboding birds? And Remus
seeing six vultures versus his brother's twelve seems
like a better omen.

How do you differentiate a good omen from a
bad omen?

And just what is an omen in the first place?

Could there be some kind of deception in the Romulus and Remus story?

Why do people only know the part of the legend
in which they were suckled by a she-wolf and not
the other more brutal part, in which one killed the
other for a reason even more vile than what led Cain
to kill Abel?

I wouldn't know how to answer these questions,
but because of them I named that night the "night of
omens." It's true that the first of them emerged the

night before, after I snorted cocaine and found the clue to Camila. And for that reason I gladly accepted more the next night, another snort while we were driving, Duilio and me, to the Cubatão casino. If that was merely an excuse I made up to snort more cocaine without being bothered by my conscience, the fact remains that I gathered new information in the casino that brought me even closer to Camila.

2

This is not the place for a discourse on the casino, which in every way reminded me of Las Vegas: spectacularly fake and poorly constructed; worn velvet curtains, croupiers in rented tuxedos, and women smiling stupid grimaces of joy, generous necklines, and a fog of tobacco. The same musty odor hovered there that I had smelled at the Dervish, but in the casino there was an effort to make the atmosphere seem somehow more sophisticated.

In any case, the first omen (good? bad?) that led me to Camila's address took place around one of the roulette tables. A dark-complexioned girl with long hair, wearing a black dress that revealed a voluptuous décolletage, caught my attention. She kissed a pile of chips and deposited them on the number 3. Then she shouted, "Three is my lucky number! It's going to be 3!"

The croupier with ears like open taxicab doors spun the wheel. All eyes were fixed on the mystic dance of the small roulette ball. Before it could decide on a number, guided by the strange and inscrutable power of fate, I noticed one of the gamblers around the table. The man, practically identical to Khalid the Bedouin, wasn't Khalid. Maybe he was Tufik, Khalid's brother. His being there made a certain sense. Or not. What if men were also an illusion? Could that be Tufik's theory? It was necessary to investigate further.

Suddenly an explosion of monosyllables brought to everyone's attention back to the dark woman with long hair and voluptuous décolletage. She rejoiced: "I knew it was going to be 3, I knew it!"

Could that be another omen? The woman had won at roulette! If that wasn't a good omen, what could be?

A good omen for her or for me?

Could omens, like women, be illusory?

The metaphysics of it overwhelmed me, but it was necessary to get to work. I went over to the bar intending to start the investigation my way, which is to say with the bartender. And then, to my surprise, the bartender himself was an omen. I knew him. His name was Tadeshi, a Nisei, approximately twenty years old and a fifth-rate con man I'd met some months before on an extortion case. He wasn't actively involved, he'd just transported the correspondence and picked up the payments; that was why Dora and I had decided not to report him, in exchange for information that might lead us to the head of the gang, a crook known as "the Japanese." When the case was solved, we suggested to Tadeshi that he drop out of sight for a time, as he might be targeted for reprisals for having snitched on the gang. And now I found him there, like a buzzard, serving drinks to customers at the Cubatão casino. A good or a bad omen? I put on a cynical happy face.

"Tadeshi, it's good to see an old friend again!"

He didn't display the least bit of joy upon recognizing me. "Working around here?" he asked, apparently annoyed.

"No, I'm on vacation, spending some of the money you guys extorted from that millionaire." (The gang had gotten hold of photos of the millionaire having sex with an underage male prostitute and threatened to make the pictures public unless he came up with a hefty sum.)

"Congratulations," he responded sarcastically.

"So this is where you found honest work?"

"I never said I'd look for honest work. I said I'd look for work; the honest part is up to you." Tadeshi moved away to tend to a couple who were already halfway through a bottle of Grants. He soon returned with an expression that suggested he knew I had him in my hands. "What's happening, Bellini, what do you want?"

"Two pieces of information," I replied. "First: do you know a dancer named Camila? She's been working here for a short time, less than a month." I was getting tired of always repeating the same story.

"I don't know nobody's name. There's orders from Mr. Focca for the dancers and musicians not to mix with other employees. We don't have any contact with them."

"Mr. Focca?" I said.

"Abel Focca, the owner of the place. His son Caruso is the one who decides who works and who doesn't. The old man just handles the dough. But Caruso doesn't do nothing without Abel's order." He brought his lips close to my ear: "Caruso is an asshole."

"Abel Focca," I said, "what a lovely name."

"Focca's a very, very clever guy."

"I wasn't referring to *Focca*; I was talking about Abel."

"Abel?"

I didn't answer, but Abel Focca was my new omen. It would be difficult to explain to Tadeshi that, just as Abel had been assassinated by Cain, Remus had also been killed by Romulus. Which made both of us, Abel Focca and Remo Bellini, two survivors.

"And where can I find Abel Focca?" I asked.

"Right here, next floor up."

I ordered a Jack Daniel's. I remembered Khalid's look-alike. That was the second piece of information I was looking for. "Tadeshi, who's that Arab-looking guy with the black hair and mustache, playing roulette?"

"He isn't playing, he's supervising. That's Tufik Tureg, the casino's administrator."

"He works for Focca?"

Tadeshi nodded. I drank the Jack Daniel's and said I wanted to meet Abel Focca. Tadeshi called over a muscular dark-skinned bouncer named Adolfo to accompany me.

"What do I owe you for the whiskey?" I asked, pointing a finger at the empty glass.

"Don't be silly," Tadeshi replied with a smirk. "Friends don't pay."

3

I followed Adolfo down deserted corridors and up empty staircases, through what looked like the private administrative area of the casino.

I reflected on the brothers Khalid and Tufik Tureg, one at the Dervish and the other at the casino, and wondered if they were related to Dr. Rafidjian and Ana Cíntia-Camila-Dinéia, the three-in-one dancer.

I didn't find an answer and went on following Adolfo.

We walked down a gloomy hallway and stopped in front of a door with a nameplate that read: *Abel Focca.* Another security man stood there, and Adolfo explained that I wanted to speak with Mr. Focca. The guy asked me to raise my arms and frisked me like a natural cop. He removed the Beretta and with his other hand knocked softly on the door. An impatient voice said, "Come in!"

The sentinel opened the door carefully and gestured to Adolfo, who said subserviently, "Mr. Focca, this man would like to speak with you."

Abel Focca was an enormous man of almost seventy. His cheeks hung from his face, making him look like an overweight dog, and he wore small glasses balanced on the tip of his nose and sported an unexpected ponytail. Sitting behind a desk covered with bills, receipts, and invoices, he directed a quick look my way and asked: "Federal or state *polith*?" I noticed he lisped.

"Federal. Agent Labelle." It was an old trick.

Presenting myself as an agent of the federal police was normally the easiest way to get information out of criminals. Of course, having to pass as a cop is always an uncomfortable task, but Agent Labelle, a fictitious character created by Dora, was an amusing alter ego, cynical and amoral.

"Adolfo, *clothe* the door and wait *outthide*," he said, peering at me over his glasses. "*Mithter* Labelle, your *paperth*, *pleathe.*"

"It's not cool to ask a police officer for his documents, Mr. Focca. Besides which, I'm not in the habit of carrying a badge on special missions."

"Our *paymenths* to the federal *polith* are up to date. If you're here after my money—"

"I don't want money. Just some information."

"You *guyth* always want *thomething* or other."

"I'm looking for a dancer named Camila. I have reason to believe she's working for you."

I noted that Focca resembled a prematurely aged baby. He pressed two buttons on the interphone hidden under papers on his desk.

"*Carutho*, come here," he ordered.

While we waited in silence for Caruso, observing Focca's flaccid countenance, I recalled our similarity as survivors: Remo and Abel, the murdered brothers. Could Abel have a brother named Cain?

Caruso eventually came in, and I observed he was a younger and fatter replica of his father. Abel explained the situation to his son and concluded by saying, "The *dethishon* is up to you, *thon.*"

Caruso replied ceremoniously, "Yes sir." He

didn't lisp. He gestured for me to follow him, and Abel Focca didn't go to the trouble of saying goodbye.

We went through a door into another room, smaller and full of files. There were two desks, and at one of them a woman was chewing gum and typing frenetically. She looked at me without interrupting her task. Caruso sat down and invited me to do likewise, pointing to a chair in front of his desk. I sat down.

"The problem, Labelle, is that here we're sticklers for the rules. All our contacts with the federal police are done through Agent Flecha. You must know Agent Flecha . . ."

I remained expressionless. This could be a trap. Incredible how I acted with such confidence under a false identity.

Caruso continued: "I can't set a precedent."

"But it's an irrelevant piece of information," I argued.

Caruso wavered. He glanced at one of the filing cabinets and I thought for a moment I would emerge victorious from that absurd pantomime. But then he turned back to me and said decisively: "No. Rules are rules. Not without Flecha's authorization. Ask him to call me, or bring a written request signed by him. Now, if you'll excuse me . . ."

It was ridiculous to have to deal with bureaucracy in a situation like this.

"One last question, Caruso." I shouldn't have done it, but I did: "Does your father have a brother named Cain?"

"Cain? Who told you that? My father's brother is named Arturo. Arturo Focca."

It clearly wasn't turning out to be an advantageous night for Agent Labelle.

After retrieving my Beretta from the sentinel, I was led by Adolfo to the ground floor. I would have to think of something else.

A Jack Daniel's, for instance.

4

I was trying to avoid taking even more risks, but it was becoming necessary.

Back with Tadeshi, who served me sullenly, I found out that Caruso usually came down from his office shortly before the "main show," around eleven, when the orchestra was playing and the dancers were doing a *Tropical Follies* number.

"Caruso shows up a little before start of the show, orders a whiskey, and does PR during the first musical number. Sometimes he stays till the second one. Then he returns to his office and doesn't leave till late, after all the employees have gone. Everybody but the security people, of course."

"Of course," I said. "What type of PR does he do?"

"Sucking up to customers, hugging the million-aires and kissing the hands of their wives, lighting their cigars, laughing at their jokes . . . But it's all real fast. His bag is upstairs, doing the books. The one handling things down here is Tufik."

"And who's Caruso's secretary?"

"Some ex-hooker, I don't know her name. After her days as a prostitute, she became the man's typist."

"Does she go with Caruso during the show?"

"Course not. The woman never leaves the office. If she did, she might scare the clientele."

Tadeshi was beckoned by customers. The couple with the Grants had already emptied the bottle and, to everyone's surprise, ordered another. I checked my watch: 9:30.

When he returned, Tadeshi said, "Look. You'd better circulate. Too many people here, and I'm fucked if they find out I'm passing along information."

"My dear man, for old times' sake, one last question. Who handles security out back?"

"Out back? That's Rocco."

"Who is Rocco?"

"He barks and has four legs."

"Tadeshi, my darling, I'm in no mood for jokes."

"I'm serious. Rocco is a dog. A mastiff trained to kill anything that moves."

"You mean the security for the rear of the casino is a dog?"

"It's not that. The watchmen patrol there every ten minutes. The problem is they have their hands full here inside. Nothing happens back there."

I became pensive. Tadeshi turned away, but I called him back: "Last question."

"You've used up your quota," he said.

"It's a question that won't get you in trouble, I swear."

"You're sure it's the last one?"

"A detective's word."

From his expression, I could tell he didn't find the joke funny.

I asked: "What's the first song in the show?"

He looked at me incredulously. It was the easiest question of the night. "'New York, New York.'"

Before leaving, I ordered a steak sandwich, rare, to go, and drank a large cup of black coffee while I was waiting for it.

5

Duilio parked the car on a dark side street some three hundred meters from the casino. From there it was possible to see the lights and hear the noise from the clandestine establishment.

"You sure this is where you want me to stop, boss?"

"Exactly. I want you to wait here for me, head-lights off, in silence. If there's a problem, blow the horn."

I set out through the thicket, in the direction of the casino, carrying the cold sandwich in a bag. Aside from some puddles that soaked my shoes, socks, and pants, it wasn't hard to get to the wall that separated the casino from the dark woods.

I wasn't enjoying this expedition through the Mata Atlântica, but after all I was a detective. I thought about calling Caruso and passing myself off as Agent Flecha, but it would be too easy to unmask me. I wasn't even sure there really was a Flecha. Very likely Caruso had made up the story to test me. And I didn't want to risk losing the lead to Camila, especially now that I had a competitor of the opposite sex (I would never again use the term "the weaker sex" after a year working with Lobo).

I climbed a tree about twenty meters from the casino wall. It took considerable effort, and I grew desperate at the thought of still having to scale two walls before arriving at my destination. The bag was tucked into my waist, between my pants and my belly. I noticed that lately my belly had been expanding against my will.

From the top of the tree I could see the open win-dow of Caruso's office. He was moving from side to side and the secretary remained seated, typing away. Through the neighboring window I spotted Abel Focca asleep on a sofa. The lights were on. My watch read 10:15.

In the yard, Rocco the watchdog was also sleeping, looking disturbingly similar to Abel.

A security guard strolled by, smoking a cigarette. Rocco raised an ear, threatened to open an eye, and went back to sleep. Everything very calm.

Half an hour passed. I was beginning to catch Rocco's and Abel's drowsiness when I noticed movement in Caruso's room. Adolfo entered, Caruso stood up and tightened the knot of his tie. They left. The secretary continued to concentrate on her typewriter. My watch said 10:55.

Time to act.

I carefully descended the tree, unwrapped the sandwich, and discarded the paper and both slices of bread. I approached the wall, holding the reddish piece of meat, then slipped it into my jacket pocket. With the Beretta tucked into my waistband, the same place the sandwich had been before, I waited.

At exactly 11:14 (I looked at my watch), the orchestra attacked the first chords of "New York, New York." That was my cue. I screwed the silencer onto my pistol, quickly scaled the wall, but as I was about to leap to the ground, there was Rocco, leaning against the wall with his front paws, growling and barking in my direction. I threw him the cold steak in hopes he would leave me alone, but he showed no interest in the meat. Rocco went on barking, threatening me with a collection of sharp white teeth. I had no alternative: I used the Beretta for the first time, shooting him twice, to the strains of "New York, New York." One bullet caught him between the eyes, the other in the throat. He fell on his side, shuddered, grunted, and rested his shattered head over a pool of blood and saliva. This business was getting to be too hairy for my taste.

Then I ran to the downspout, climbed it, crept along the roof, and entered Caruso's office like in a movie: I swung my body inside in a pendular motion, and before the secretary could comprehend what was happening, I greeted her with the sight of the Beretta pointing at her forehead.

"In the bathroom!" I ordered. "Open your mouth and I'll kill you."

I locked her in the bathroom, locked the doors leading to the corridor and to Abel Focca's office, and dashed to the filing cabinets. Downstairs they were still on "New York, New York."

I started my search with the C folders but discovered they were filed by surname, of course. I was obliged to check the names of all the casino's employees. Luckily, there was only one Camila; I found her under the letter *G: Camila Garcia. Rua Tratado de Tordesilhas, #63. Ponta da Praia, Santos.*

The file contained several entries documenting days she had missed work, including that same day, May 19. *Reason: illness.* At that moment, someone tried to open the hallway door. Finding it locked, they began to knock loudly.

"Mirna! What's going on? Open the door!" I recognized Caruso's voice.

I was already in the yard, running for the wall, when I heard Mirna yelling for help. The orchestra was playing another piece, one I didn't recognize. I heard shouts coming from the window, followed by shots.

Before jumping over the wall I glanced at Rocco's corpse and found it odd that I didn't feel any remorse at all. That was the last of the omens.

After the girl who won at roulette, Tufik, Tadeshi, Abel, and Rocco, the best thing for me was to stop snorting powder and concentrate on work.

6

In the car, on the way to Camila Garcia's address, Duilio offered me some blow. I had come to a decision and said, "No thanks, I'm not going to snort more."

"Why's that, boss?"

"Because when I snort, I have the impression that everything makes sense."

"How so?"

"I have the feeling that everything is trying to say something, and what's worse, that everything's trying to say something to *me*, you understand?"

"No," he replied, holding the steering wheel with one hand while managing a quick, precise sniff without taking his eyes off the road.

"It's simple: when I do cocaine, I get the impression that every happening is offering me leads to other happenings, as if everything happens because it has to happen, as if life is nothing but a simple succession of preprogrammed happenings."

"And what *is* life like, then?" he asked.

"I don't know, I just don't want to think it's possible to predict the next step, you understand?"

"No. That sounds like cokehead talk to me."

"Fine, let's drop it. Do you know where Rua Tratado de Tordesilhas is?"

"No, but we'll find it."

I was tired, wet, and scratched up. But I felt happy at having shot a dog. I wasn't going to worry anymore about omens, nor about brothers who kill brothers.

Maybe the cocaine was getting me into depths that shouldn't be plumbed.

* * *

When we reached Ponta da Praia, a district in Santos, we roamed around a little until we found Rua Tratado de Tordesilhas. Duilio parked on a cross street so as not to attract attention and waited for me there.

Tratado de Tordesilhas is only two blocks long, starting at Avenida Beira-Mar and ending in a small square. The street consists of houses, a grocery, a butcher shop, a pharmacy, and a bakery. At that hour, midnight, all the commercial establishments were closed and there was no one around.

House #63 was a small triplex, with no garden and a minuscule terrace and a door with a shutter. There was a light on inside. I stayed there on the opposite sidewalk, not taking my eyes off the house. No movement. The silence was cut only by the occasional car passing on Avenida Beira-Mar.

At 1:16 a.m. the lights were turned off in the living room, but I could make out bluish reflections through the frosted glass of the shutters. Someone was watching television. I remained in position for another hour. Around two in the morning, the TV was turned off. The street was plunged into a sepulchral silence, and I was exhausted.

I woke up Duilio, who despite the cocaine was profoundly asleep in the car. And we returned to the hotel.

MAY 20

Sunday

1

There's one indispensable quality for a detective: patience.

On Sunday I spent approximately seventeen hours on my feet, from seven thirty in the morning till half past midnight, staring at that small house. During that period, I went to the Nau de Goa Bakery two or three times. It stayed open all day, till eight at night. My nourishment that day consisted of two cheese-and-salami sandwiches and a few cups of coffee. I planted the rumor that I worked for a research institute and was observing the habits of the street for a publicity agency. While I ate or talked, I kept one eye glued to the door of #63.

Early in the morning, around eight thirty, a man who appeared to be past seventy, wearing a beret and wool sweater despite the heat, came out of the house and walked to the bakery. He bought milk and some rolls. Later, at 2:38 p.m. to be exact, the same man, still wearing the beret but without the sweater, went to the pharmacy and returned with a small package in his hands. He limped slightly. He had the relaxed look of the retired, was unshaven, and wore wrinkled clothes. Later, thanks to a talkative saleslady, I learned he had purchased two over-the-counter items—Plasil (antinausea medication) and Voltaren (an analgesic for rheumatic pains). She also said he was a retired widower who lived alone. On rare occasions he would receive a visit from one of his children. She didn't know whether at the moment anyone else was there. He often bought Voltaren, but as far as she knew, it was the first time for Plasil. She didn't know the widower's name. She called him "sir."

The only time that Sunday when I took my eyes off the house were the minutes spent in the bathroom at the Nau de Goa. I couldn't risk pissing in the street and calling the attention of the entire neighborhood.

2

Around seven that evening I was beset by a bout of paranoia: was Camila even inside the house? Was I wasting precious time on a false lead? That gal Beatriz had Dinéia's address and photos, and I still had nothing tangible, just an address. Was I chasing a ghost? Who was Ana Cíntia-Dinéia-Camila? And who was Beatriz?

I thought about Fatima, the only real woman I'd met in the last three days. And what about the kiss we had shared? What nonsense was that?

Before I started hearing my father saying how stupid I was and my ex-wife complaining about my adolescent fantasies, I decided to take action. I hid the camera inside my jacket (besides patience, detectives need pockets) and strode resolutely toward #63. I rang the bell. The elderly man with the beret opened the shutter and said in an ill-humored Spanish accent: "What do you want?"

I took a deep breath. "Good afternoon, sir. I'm here on behalf of Caruso Focca with a message for Camila Garcia."

"What is it?"

"He would like to know whether she's going to return to work. She's missed a lot of days and he needs to know what her plans are."

"Just a moment."

He returned a few minutes later. "She says not to worry, next weekend she'll be back." And he closed the shutter.

I resumed my position across the street and waited there until the light from the TV went out at around twelve thirty a.m. I walked for several blocks before finding a taxi. I had dispensed with Duilio because I didn't want to snort any more coke and because I no longer needed to be driven around the city. Besides which, it was wise to save money, which Dora would appreciate.

Dora. The previous night, when I called and gave my report on my adventure in the casino, she said, referring to the death of the dog Rocco: "Well done. I can't stand mastiffs or Pekingese." About my discovery of Camila's address, she commented: "The fish took the bait, now we just have to wait for the right time to haul in the catch."

When I returned to the hotel the following night, I barely had the strength to relate the facts of that frustrating Sunday. At the end of the call I said, "The fish took the bait but doesn't want to show its face."

"Don't worry," she replied. "It's just a matter of time. A short time. By Wednesday this case will be solved, mark my words."

I remembered Dinéia (had I ever really forgotten her?) and asked Dora about Beatriz's photos.

"They're excellent. Dinéia fits Don Quixote's description of Ana Cíntia perfectly. Now we're going to wait for the mysterious Camila. Wednesday night, I guarantee it, you, Beatriz, and I will have dinner at a restaurant and celebrate with French champagne, on Rafidjian's dime."

Without knowing where she got such confidence from, I blacked out from exhaustion as soon as I hung up the phone.

MAY 21

Monday

1

At eight a.m. I was on Rua Tratado de Tordesilhas, armed with my camera, my eyes glued to the door of #63. It was Monday and the street was busier than the day before. To amuse myself during the endless hours of waiting, I took my Walkman this time and listened to some classics by Big Bill Broonzy. "When I Been Drinking" has always been my favorite.

At eight thirty the man in the beret and sweater walked with his slight limp toward the bakery and returned with the same container of milk and package of bread as the day before. I hid behind a tree, which was ridiculous: according to Dashiell Hammett, only fictitious detectives hide behind trees.

In the following hours nothing happened except I traded Big Bill Broonzy for Blind Willie McTell. At three o'clock, as I mentally reviewed my memoirs, the door to #63 slowly opened.

There she was: Camila leaving her hole. I had landed the fish at last.

She was fragile and ethereal (her white skin contrasted with the violence of the afternoon sun). Her eyes were deep-set and her body was simultaneously harmonious and aggressive. She was wearing a sleeveless black T-shirt that emphasized the voluptuous swell of her breasts and a short skirt, black with white polka dots. On her feet, a pair of brown leather sandals with laces up to midcalf. I grabbed my camera and took almost an entire roll without pausing between shots.

Camila seemed distant, divorced from what was happening around her, and didn't even notice me, the lunatic who was photographing her from the opposite sidewalk.

She went into the pharmacy. While she was inside I changed rolls of film.

As she headed back to the house, Camila struck me as being inebriated, in a torpor I couldn't read. I took some more photos. She entered #63, closed the door, and I ran to the bakery.

I ordered a beer and drank almost the whole bottle in a single gulp. I celebrated my success quietly by eating a sandwich and drinking another beer.

Then I caught a taxi and returned to the hotel.

When I arrived, Sintra told me: "There's an urgent message for you."

"What is it?"

"To call Dora Lobo. Right away."

I went up to my room still brimming with satisfaction. I wavered between writing the report or phoning Lobo, but since she had called, which wasn't typical, I decided to get back to her before doing anything else.

Rita answered the phone with her shrill voice and told me to hold for a moment. Right away I heard Dora's deep and stern voice: "Bellini, come back immediately."

"Why?" I asked.

"Dr. Rafidjian has been murdered."

"What?"

"Dr. Rafidjian was murdered."

2

Immediately after hanging up I got in a taxi and made it to the office in São Paulo around six that evening.

I found Dora sitting at her desk. An empty glass with traces of port wine and an ashtray overflowing with Tiparillo butts revealed her mood. In front of the desk, sitting in the armchair I usually occupied, was a slim young woman with short dark hair and round glasses, also sipping wine. I noticed that her lips were moistened with port. Both women looked at me, surprised. Dora rose and came toward me with her arms spread.

"Bellini, dear." Pulling me by the hands. "This is Beatriz."

Beatriz stood up and smiled with her large mouth in an angular face. But what caught my attention were her long legs and her small, firm breasts.

I greeted her. She said: "I'm finally meeting the famous Bellini."

We laughed nervously, betraying a suspicious excitement. Dora suggested we sit down, then went to the liquor cabinet and poured another glass of port and offered me a Scotch.

"You're going to need it, the story is kind of rough . . ."

Beatriz watched me out of the corner of her eye, and when our gazes crossed she seemed to be wrestling with some enigma created by my presence. I took a healthy swallow and became all ears. Dora lit another Tiparillo and assumed the expression she displayed only when narrating a crime (and what pleasure she took in narrating a crime).

"Dr. Rafidjian was murdered today, in his office on the eleventh floor of a building for medical and dental practices, sometime between noon and one p.m. when his secretary, Dona Gláucia, went to lunch, as she does religiously every day. She's done that for years, and doubtlessly the criminal was aware of it. When she came back from her meal promptly at one o'clock, Dona Gláucia found the door open that separates the waiting room from the consultation rooms. That was totally abnormal. Upon entering the consultation area, she discovered Rafidjian's body lying in the middle of the room. He was belly-up and his face was completely disfigured; he had bled to death. She started screaming, drawing the attention of nearby offices on the same floor. The doctors who worked there confirmed that Rafidjian was dead and called the police."

Dora paused for a moment, then continued: "The initial impressions by the police are that it wasn't a burglary, as nothing was missing; and amazingly . . . the murder weapon was an umbrella, Rafidjian's own umbrella!"

"How so?" I asked, intrigued.

"Rafidjian's face was lacerated by blows struck with the point of his own umbrella, an umbrella he always carried. He even had it with him when he was here. I remember that detail very clearly, because it caught my attention: a man carrying an umbrella on a night when there wasn't the slightest threat of rain . . ."

"And the murderer, after killing the doctor, apparently poked out his eyes in a display of extreme sadism," said Beatriz with a strange, morbid (and sensual) smile.

Dora: "The police quickly interrogated all the porters, elevator operators, employees in the labs and medical offices, janitors, garage attendants, doctors, dentists, and patients about the possibility of having seen anyone suspicious entering or leaving the building during that time. They found nothing— it's a large building with numerous doctors' offices and labs with constant coming and going."

"How do you know all this?" I asked. "The crime was committed just six hours ago."

"Very simple," Dora replied. "The one heading the investigation is Boris."

Detective Boris Ferreira in the homicide division was an old acquaintance of Dora's. Although younger (around forty-five), both identified with the concept of the "ideal investigator." And Boris, despite being quite eccentric, had no peer when it came to solving complicated crimes.

"Yes," I said, "but how did he find out you were involved with Rafidjian?"

"Look, Boris's first thought when he entered the office was to go through the drawers of Rafidjian's desk. He found our contract stuck in an appointment book or something like that. He called me immediately. That was around three this afternoon.

Beatriz and I were here, checking some details in the reports. I asked her to go to the crime scene and follow the investigation. Boris wants to talk to you tomorrow morning, nine sharp, at homicide. After that, at eleven thirty, I want you and Beatriz at Don Quixote's funeral."

"Anything else?" I asked.

"Boris is intrigued. In his eighteen years as a cop he's never seen anyone killed with an umbrella."

3

Beatriz had come back from Rafidjian's office shortly before I arrived. Dora asked her to bring me up to date. She cleared her throat and said: "All the doctor's family members were there, crying and screaming. It was horrible." She took a swallow of wine. "Detective Boris let me go right away, at six in the afternoon. The crime scene squad had just gotten there and the specialists were combing for evidence. Fingerprints, hair, forensics. He said the body would be sent to the morgue for autopsy. Tomorrow or day after tomorrow at latest he should have the results . . . and the detective repeated several times: 'An umbrella, who would've thought it, an umbrella.'"

I felt like grabbing Beatriz, kissing her wine-damp lips, tearing off her clothes, and biting the nipples of her firm breasts. Dora called me back to reality, as if guessing my secret desires.

"From the looks of things we're removing ourselves from the case." She gave me a severe stare, taking on that school principal air. "Let's turn to our final obligations: Bellini, hand over the film so Rita can still get someone to develop it today. I'm curious to see Camila's face. At nine tomorrow you'll meet Boris and take him the reports and the photos of Camila and Dinéia. Afterward, you'll go with Beatriz to the doctor's funeral. I want a final report on all of it."

"Why?" I asked. "The case is over. Our client was murdered."

"Because I like to keep documents on file in unfinished cases, it's a habit," she replied.

Despite her efforts to appear pragmatic, Dora couldn't hide her frustration. Rafidjian, Ana Cíntia, Dinéia, and Camila continued to be an enigma, and Dora was always drawn to enigmas.

Deciphering them was a question of honor.

4

The mention of those names made me curious. Ana Cíntia, Camila, and Dinéia. Ana Cíntia was quite probably a pseudonym of one of the other two. Camila I already knew. I asked Beatriz and Dora to show me the photos of Dinéia. Dora took an envelope from a desk drawer and spread the photographs on its surface.

Dinéia Isidoro was young, with an earnest smile and something Indian in her features. I saw photos of Dinéia and her mother, an elderly woman with an enigmatic gaze and ravaged skin, also with Indian features. They were in a small living room with Formica furniture and, in the background, two pictures hanging on the wall. One was an image of Jesus with his heart in flames, pierced by thorns, bleeding. The other, older, showed a man and woman, newlyweds. The faces of the bride and groom were retouched, making them appear unreal and frightening despite the fact that they were smiling. Another photo showed children of various ages, all of them seemingly half-Indian, smiling. Dinéia and her mother, with serious expressions, beside the TV. Two little sisters with their hands on Dinéia's belly.

The voice of Beatriz seemed to emerge from one of the photographs: "Does Dinéia look like Camila?"

"No. It's funny how the two fit the description of Ana Cíntia but are completely different from each other."

"It's a shame to have to abandon the case just when it's starting to get interesting!" Dora's voice was like a hammer pounding on an anvil.

As if thinking aloud, Beatriz stated: "I won't lie,

I'm relieved to be off the case." She examined the photos, still on the desk. "I said I was a social worker and those people opened their house to me with total hospitality and trust. They even offered me coffee, cake, those things. I'm not cut out to be a detective, not at all."

"My dear," replied Dora gruffly, "in the majority of cases a lawyer is obliged to lie as much as or more than a detective."

I intervened: "I think we're all rattled by the situation. How about some pizza and beer—aren't you two hungry?" Silently, I congratulated myself for my presence of mind.

The atmosphere in the office had become unbearable. The corpse of Rafidjian with his eyes gouged out by an umbrella, the melancholy poverty of Dinéia and her family in that tiny house on the outskirts of Cornélio Procópio, Camila's chemically induced torpor and the limping steps of her widowed father in Santos, and most of all our frustration at not being able to do anything further with a case that became more complicated (and interesting) by the minute— had all left our nerves rubbed raw.

One feeling, however, overshadowed my frustration. It was the strange excitement that Beatriz's presence aroused in me. There was something intriguing in her apparent normality.

I couldn't explain what was going on with me, so I let the unexplainable manifest itself.

Dora, Beatriz and I ended the night at the Pizzeria Camelo, on Rua Pamplona.

We ate garlic pizza and drank beer, lots of beer. During the meal, someone bumped Beatriz's chair and her purse, which was hanging from it, fell to the floor. She bent down to pick it up and I caught a glimpse of both her breasts. The sight impressed and rattled me.

After eating, we drank some more, and by the end of the evening we were more or less resigned to the abrupt conclusion of the case. On the way back I drove Dora's car and we dropped Beatriz at her home. She lived with her mother (her parents were separated) in a two-story house in Jardins. When we said good night I muttered something like, "It was very nice to meet you," and she said, "None of that, Bellini," and then, smiling with her strange morbidity, "Tomorrow we've got a funeral to go to." That was when I felt something happening.

"Magic" was how Dora referred to the phenomenon she had just witnessed, and, vain about her capacity for observing human behavior, she didn't refrain from commenting.

She dropped me off at Baronesa de Arary.

When I was almost at the door, she called out from the car: "Get whatever information you can out of Boris. I want to know what the police think about all this."

Before going to sleep, as I lay in bed listening to Robert Johnson, the scene I kept coming back to wasn't Dinéia's Indian mother, or Camila's leather sandals, or Dora talking about Rafidjian's empty eye sockets.

It was the sight of Beatriz's breasts.

MAY 22

Tuesday

1

Boris received me promptly at nine in his cramped office on the sixth floor of the building housing the homicide division. A single window faced the wall of another building, which heightened the sensation of claustrophobia that suddenly assailed me.

Boris's walls were dirty, an indefinable white, unadorned by any picture or poster. Just the official portrait of the governor and a calendar with sayings from the Seichō-No-Ie movement. The one for May 22 was: *The sun rises on the horizon. The wise man contemplates and gives thanks.*

A small bookcase held a collection of Poe's short stories and Stevenson's *The Strange Case of Dr. Jekyll and Mr. Hyde*, side by side with Nelson Hungria's volumes of *Commentaries on the Penal Code* (which I was familiar with from Tulio Bellini's office) and phone books. Lots of phone books from various cities.

Boris was a guy with oily black hair and pale skin marked by vestiges of acne. He was wearing a coat a size too small and a yellow tie. What most caught my attention about him, however, were the square glasses with thick lenses. Although he seemed a bit absentminded, Boris was obsession personified.

I was there to provide information, but he was the one greeting me with news.

"You were in Santos looking for . . ." he consulted a sheet of paper on his desk, "Camila. Is that right?"

"Right. Camila Garcia," I answered.

"And the one in Cornélio Procópio looking for Dinéia, Dinéia Duarte Isidoro, was—" Boris turned his head in the direction of his desk.

"Beatriz," I said, before he had time to consult his notes again.

"Very good. In spite of not having any idea yet who committed the crime, I already know it was neither of the two girls."

Brilliant, I thought, *a deduction worthy of Sherlock Holmes*.

"Camila's alibi," he said, "is you, Bellini. You were surveilling her house at the approximate time of the crime, correct?"

"That's right."

"And Dinéia's is Dr. . . . Dr. . . ." He glanced at the papers on his desk. "Dr. Fragoso, from the Cornélio Procópio hospital."

"Dr. Fragoso?"

"Correct. Dinéia has been in the hospital in Cornélio Procópio since yesterday morning. She was three months pregnant, more or less, and lost the child—the fetus, I mean—in a miscarriage yesterday around noon, the probable time the crime was committed. I just found out." Boris continued perusing the notes that covered every available inch of his small desk. "She felt ill late Sunday night, bleeding that wouldn't stop. She went into the hospital early Monday morning. The fetus died, but Dinéia is all right."

I remembered the photo of Dinéia's sisters with their hands on her belly. Boris picked up a pack of cigarettes and offered me one.

"Thanks, I don't smoke."

"Good for you," he replied, raising a cigarette to his mouth and lighting it. "Okay, Bellini, tell me your story." And he blew smoke at the ceiling, staring at me.

2

I narrated the events, which were taking on new shape and becoming more complex with each passing day.

Boris jotted down the details of my account amid the chaos that reigned on his desk. Some of the names I cited warranted comments on his part: "Khalid and Tufik Tureg are con men and procurers well known to the police here in São Paulo." Another point that intrigued him was the episode in the clandestine casino in Cubatão and mention of the name Abel Focca. According to him, Focca was a "notorious mafioso" tasked with implanting branches of the Mafia throughout Brazil. Mafia bases already existed in Rio de Janeiro and Santos and would soon be in São Paulo as well, aiming to control the drug trade, gambling, and prostitution in the entire country. He was concerned about the possibility of Khalid and Tufik serving as a bridge to the mafiosi, collaborating to establish their bases in São Paulo. All of this had as its goal the conquest of South America. "This is a job for the federal police. I need to notify them," he said. "It's urgent that they find out the identity of that agent, Flecha. The police mustn't become a den of traitors."

Boris was dismayed when I told him I had killed the dog Rocco. "Poor animal," he reflected, "one more innocent victim of the Mafia's unbridled ambition."

The statements by Stone, Iório's informant, were classified as "extremely important," which meant Stone would have to spend a bit more of his precious time in the pleasant company of cops, which he'd of course love. Fatima, the odalisque with large breasts, would also be called in for a chat, and even Tadeshi, Sintra, and his son-in-law Duilio had their names added to the notes. Camila and Dinéia would be interrogated "quite rigorously," in Boris's words, "and we can be sure the mystery of Ana Cíntia Lopes will get cleared up once and for all."

I asked if he really thought Focca, or the Mafia, as well as Khalid and his brother Tufik, had any connection to the murder.

"Probably not," he replied, "but we have to consider all hypotheses. Remember, we have no clues." He quickly added: "In any case, killing with an umbrella isn't the Mafia way, you can be sure of that."

Despite my vow to stop worrying about omens and brothers who kill one another, curiosity got the better of me and I asked, "Detective, do you know Arturo Focca, Abel's brother?"

"He's a priest," Boris answered.

"A priest?"

"A Catholic priest who catechizes Indians in the Amazon. In Mafia families it's common to have one brother who's a priest."

I nodded, then asked: "What about the Rafidjian family?"

"A normal family. In homicide cases where the

victim is an unfaithful husband, the wife is always a suspect. But we don't know for sure that Rafidjian was an adulterer. Besides, the widow, Dona Sofia, has an alibi supported by her servants. At the time her husband was killed, she was at home having lunch with Silvia and Sergio, two of her children, while Samuel, the oldest, was leaving class for basketball practice at the Pinheiros Club, which he does Monday, Wednesday, and Friday. Between school and the club he stopped at a luncheonette for a quick meal."

"What about the rest of the family—parents, siblings, et cetera?"

"A family of well-to-do Armenian businessmen." He put out his cigarette. "They're close, ordinary, nothing that arouses suspicion."

"Did Rafidjian have enemies?"

"No. He was respected in his social circle, despite being a bit arrogant like most surgeons."

"And Dona Glaucia?" I asked.

"What about Dona Glaucia?"

"Do you suspect her?"

"Dona Glaucia, Rafidjian's secretary?"

"Yeah."

"You're crazy." He shook his head. "Have you seen Dona Glaucia?"

"No."

"Then forget it. Dona Glaucia is a nearsighted, nervous little old lady."

"Maybe she was in love with the doctor," I ventured.

"Bellini, I've been in homicide for eighteen years, and I can assure you that a weak elderly woman couldn't manage to kill a man of his size using nothing but an umbrella."

"But umbrellas are typical weapons for little old ladies."

He didn't take these comments seriously (and I didn't censure him for it). He lit another cigarette and stared at his notes. The photos of Camila and Dinéia, which I had brought him in a manila envelope, were spread now out on the desk, mixed in with the other papers.

"It's the umbrella that makes this case exceptional," said Boris. "Maybe your inexperience doesn't allow you to recognize how odd this is. An umbrella—who would kill a man using an umbrella?"

He posed this question without any expectation that I could answer it. But I tried: "Someone who didn't premeditate the crime."

"What?"

"Anyone who intended to kill Rafidjian would surely have carried a weapon."

"That's possible," said Boris. "But a crime always

has unfathomable subtleties. Imagine that the criminal would like the police to think precisely along those lines and, knowing that Rafidjian kept an umbrella in his office, decided to kill him with it merely to throw us off the trail. Wouldn't that be plausible?"

I had to agree.

I checked my watch: 10:48. I asked Boris if he was on his way to Rafidjian's funeral, scheduled for 11:30.

"I'll meet you at the cemetery," he answered. "I have some other appointments before then."

I said goodbye, and he grunted an "okay" worthy of a zombie and went on looking at the photos of Camila and Dinéia on his desk as if nothing else in the universe existed.

As I headed down the corridor, I noticed two stern men coming toward me from the opposite direction. I was already by the elevator door when they accosted me. The thinner of the two said: "Your name, please."

"Bellini." Because I felt cornered, I added without thinking, "Remo Bellini."

"Profession?"

"Private detective. Why?" Cops, I suspected.

"You work with Detective Lobo?"

"Yes. Why the interrogation?"

The fatter of the two suddenly pointed a camera at me and shot several pictures point-blank.

"Shit!" I pushed them away and ran toward the stairs.

On the street, I made sure I wasn't being followed. I felt a cold pit in my stomach. From shame, not fear. I had been fooled by two reporters who looked like Laurel and Hardy, and that made me a perfect idiot.

3

Cemetery Peace, in the Morumbi district, is one of those American-style cemeteries with a huge expanse of grass dotted by horizontal marble gravestones here and there.

The sensation I felt when I arrived was one of vastness and peace of mind, quite different from the claustrophobia I always felt when I visited the Bellini family plot in Consolação Cemetery, a traditional Catholic cemetery that was a true city of the dead.

Family and friends were at the wake, gathered around the casket, sealed because Rafidjian's face had been destroyed by the umbrella, which now had the status of a deadly weapon.

The casket was carried by six men; the handles at the front were held by a tall, thin young man and a short, plump boy. Both were weeping openly, and I deduced they were Samuel and Sergio, the dead man's sons. The remaining handles were manned by three middle-aged guys (who looked like brothers or cousins of the doctor) and an older gentleman with white hair, Ivan Boudeni, the renowned heart surgeon and professor at the São Paulo Medical School. The widow, Sofia, maintained her composure as she walked behind the casket, embracing her daughter, a fifteen-year-old who was crying incessantly.

At the sepulchre, my attention was drawn to a gravedigger who wore Ray-Ban sunglasses, a felt hat, and faded jeans. His appearance contrasted starkly with Rafidjian's relatives and friends, all of whom were dressed elegantly and discreetly. A fat old lady was crying scandalously. *Our Don Quixote's mother*, Dora would say.

It seemed as if everyone there was acting and dressing as one might expect, given the circumstances. Anyone who might provide a clue as to Rafidjian's other life, if there actually was another Rafidjian unknown to us, didn't show up. No one there resembled a prostitute, pimp, gambler, or even a simple assassin. The oddest person there, other than the gravedigger in Ray-Bans, was Boris in his Coke-bottle glasses, his undersized shabby coat, and yellow tie.

Beatriz observed the burial from a distance. Dona Glaucia, Rafidjian's secretary, was comforted the entire time by the doctor's relatives. Her disconsolate look confirmed my suspicion that she was in love with her boss.

I noticed that Boris was watching me watch her. He shook his head as if to say, *Give up, Bellini.* I also noticed a tall, chunky biracial woman who was consoling the younger children, Sergio and Silvia. By her unpretentious appearance and the intimacy she displayed with the Rafidjians, I concluded she was one of those servants who end up becoming part of the family.

I went over to Beatriz and invited her to have a drink in the cemetery bar. They didn't sell alcoholic beverages, so we had to content ourselves with coffee.

She was beautiful in the bright light of that May morning. Her wide mouth, dark hair, slim body, her small and enticing breasts. Our conversation was strange, a bit tense, and the principal topic was death.

Maybe it's because we were in a cemetery, but I had the unmistakable feeling that for Beatriz sex and death were inseparable.

MAY 23

Wednesday

I saw my startled face printed in the largest-circulation paper in São Paulo: *Detective Remo Bellini of the Lobo Detective Agency, after his statement at the homicide division, where he explained why they had been hired by the murdered doctor.* One of the items dealing with the crime bore the title: *Detective was investigating a prostitute the surgeon was in love with.*

Press coverage focused on the thesis that Rafidjian was a happily married man who led a double life, secretly meeting a prostitute in the downtown area of the city. The name of the prostitute, however, did not appear in any of the papers. The reason, according to reporters, was that the police refused to divulge the woman's identity in order not to hinder the investigation. I experienced a nervous calm, if there is such a thing.

The police didn't manage to sit on the information for long, and the following day I read in all the papers the name I had been living with: *Ana Cíntia Lopes.*

That pained me as if someone had broken into my home and stolen a nude photo of an ex-girlfriend. I also read about Camila Garcia and Dinéia Isidoro, and it was strange to see their names printed in those small, impersonal letters.

But what irritated me the most was reading the name *Remo* in the paper.

The dumbstruck, imbecilic expression caught on my face in the photograph made me feel like crap. I looked like a complete idiot to whom no one in his or her right mind should trust a mission requiring a modicum of intelligence.

Besides which, in the picture I appeared several pounds overweight, and I hadn't even been eating junk food.

MAY 24

Thursday

1

Lobo was frowning when I entered her office looking for a little psychological comforting. She was in the habit of saying that any time a detective's work becomes public, he has failed. "The detective's work is secret as a matter of principle."

She couldn't stand seeing her name published in all the papers around town. It was a significant defeat.

I invited her to have some coffee in order to take her mind off it, but she preferred to go up to the top floor for a few Scotches at the Itália Terrace and contemplate the city from above. After two rounds, accompanied by shelled peanuts, her scowl melted away.

"Well, Bellini," she said, "the game's over." She lit a Tiparillo.

"What's your conclusion?" I asked.

"There was already a mystery behind everything, even before the murder." She blew smoke out of her nostrils. "Some of the facts don't add up."

"For example?"

"I've analyzed the reports." She gestured with the hand holding the cigarette. "There are certain contradictions: I find it odd that Stone and Fatima didn't recognize Rafidjian. Look, if Camila or Dinéia really did have a relationship of some kind with the doctor, we could expect they'd have commented about it to the other workers. Rafidjian was too peculiar to go unnoticed in an environment where gossip is a means of bonding."

She took a sip of the whiskey and gazed pensively at the cigarette in the ashtray. "When he came to me," she continued, "Rafidjian said he had investigated the Dervish on his own, along with other clubs, interrogating customers and employees about Ana Cíntia's whereabouts. No one cited that fact, none of the people you contacted mentioned it. The bartender at the Dervish said nothing about it, nor did Fatima or Stone, nobody said a single word."

"Maybe I was unlucky and investigated the wrong people. After all, my investigation wasn't all that comprehensive." I felt a certain pleasure in countering her.

Dora shook her head.

"So what's your hypothesis then?" I asked.

"I don't have a hypothesis. I'm just not convinced that Don Quixote was simply a voyeur who fell in love with a hooker from the Dervish."

"Why not?"

"Because he was murdered."

2

I asked the waiter for two more drinks. We were silent for some moments. When he brought the drinks, even before clearing away the empty glasses, he said: "You're working on the case of that doctor killed with an umbrella, aren't you?"

Dora was furious, and I, fearing she would commit some incivility, jumped in: "You read that in the paper?"

"No, I saw it just now on TV, *News at Noon*."

"Yes," I said, "we *were*. Now it's in the hands of the police."

"Could I get your autograph?" He took a pad of paper from his pocket along with the pen he used to write down orders and offered them to Dora. She remained motionless, disconcerted, and I grabbed the sheet of paper and scrawled my signature on it. The waiter went away grateful.

"That's success, Dora—you have to learn to deal with it."

"A detective's success is complete anonymity," she shot back.

"It's time for you to stop being so dogmatic and begin enjoying the laurels of glory."

Dora limited her response to a scathing look.

We took a few sips, and I returned to the subject: "Seriously, do you think the doctor's death has anything to do with the Tureg brothers or the Mafia?"

"I don't think so," she answered distantly.

"Is that it? 'I don't think so'? Tell me, Dora, what did I do for you to go so cold on me?"

"Speaking of cold," she said, assuming that schoolmaster air of hers, "I think it's best for you to stop drinking, cold turkey."

"What are you talking about?"

"I'm talking about you stopping drinking."

"And since when do you decide when and how much I should drink?" I asked, feigning indignation.

"Since now, sonny boy. We've got a new case."

"A new case?"

"Yes. Enough drama. Dr. Rafidjian is a thing of the past, I've turned the page, it's over. Now it's just something for the media."

"Are you serious?" She definitely knew how to surprise me.

"Look, Bellini, we've got to work. Are you going to disrupt the normal flow of life because Dr.

Rafidjian"—she pronounced the name in a playful manner—"was killed?"

I took a generous swallow of whiskey and asked, "What the hell kind of case is it?"

"A piece of cake. All you have to do is follow a guy."

"Who?"

"A businessman. Pompilio Nagra. His partner, Fabian Fegri, suspects he's passing confidential information to competitors. Professional betrayal. All you have to do is tail Pompilio twenty-four hours a day and write down where he's going."

3

It may have been easy, but it was also going to be really boring. Following a businessman who was betraying his partner was as compelling to me as going to the dentist.

We paid our check at the Itália Terrace and went down to the office to discuss details of the case. Before I left, Dora asked, blatantly contradicting herself, "Did Boris make any comment about that foreign partner of Camila's?"

"Boris didn't comment about anything," I replied. "He kept obsessing over the photos of Dinéia and Camila and didn't even say goodbye when I left. Boris is a little bit unbalanced, isn't he?"

"Unbalanced enough to be considered the best cop in homicide."

"Fine, but as far as I recall, he didn't mention anything about a foreigner. What exactly are you trying to say?" My brain was kind of scrambled from the whiskey.

"I'm saying you need to stop drinking. Concentrate, Remo Bellini."

When she called me Remo I knew things weren't going very well.

She went on, impatiently: "Remember your conversation with the informant at the Bisteca d'Ouro? That little piece of shit said the last time he saw Camila she was performing with a foreigner called Miguel or Manuel. He even referred to the show as 'fabulous.'"

"That idiot probably thinks a yo-yo is the most fabulous thing in the world."

"No jokes, kiddo."

"Sorry, but I can't take a guy seriously who says the drug is 'real cheap.'"

"I'm not saying you should take Stone seriously, I just want to know if Boris made any comment about that Miguel or Manuel."

"I do remember. Miguel or Manuel. Boris didn't say anything about him. Why should he?"

"No reason," she answered. "The name came into my head, that's all."

"I thought you said the Rafidjian case is a thing of the past."

She smiled and turned on the record player she kept in her office. The room was invaded by one of her symphonies, the signal that our conversation had come to an end.

4

I went home and couldn't get Beatriz out of my head.

What was this—love at first sight? Lack of a woman?

I made a sandwich with the last of the cream cheese and put on a Muddy Waters tape. As he sang "Good Morning, Little Schoolgirl," I imagined Beatriz innocently walking to class with her law books clutched to the small breasts I had glimpsed in the pizzeria.

What was this, late-manifesting adolescent deliriums?

"Tell your mother and your father, I once was a schoolboy too."

I checked my watch: 7:45. I decided to call her.

"Hello? Is Beatriz in?"

"No." The voice sounded like an older woman. "Who's calling?"

"It's Bellini. Remo Bellini." Why did I say *Remo*? I wasn't in the habit of doing that, except when I was very nervous.

"I don't know what time she'll be back, Bellini. Do you want to leave a message?" The voice suddenly wasn't that of an older woman, just one who was . . . more mature.

"No thanks. Just say I called. Goodbye."

"Goodbye."

I hung up. Every time I fell in love, I wove fantasies about the mother of the woman I was in love with. Since childhood. The woman I had spoken to on the phone was probably Beatriz's mother, and in my imagination she had already taken on the form of a more experienced Beatriz, more maternal and more understanding. I've always had a weakness for older women. I collapsed on the sofa and surrendered myself to daydreams and the sound of Jimmy Reed.

Women are even more of an illusion on the phone, I thought. What would Khalid say if he knew how often I fell in love just by hearing a pretty voice?

5

I fell asleep.

I dreamed of a black man in dark glasses, walking through a cane field. He wasn't Brazilian, he was American.

The phone rang. I picked it up, despite not being fully awake.

"Hello?"

It was a woman's voice. I thought it was Beatriz, but I wasn't sure.

"Who's speaking?" I asked, still half asleep.

It was Fatima. I woke up fully.

"Fatima. It's been a long time."

"Right, now you're famous, you're in the papers and on TV every day."

"That's true, but it's not good. The clients might lose confidence."

"No. Publicity's always a good thing."

"So then, Fatima?"

"So then, what?"

"Why'd you call me?"

"I called because you owe me one, remember?"

That took me by surprise. I really did owe her one. The problem was finding out what she meant by "one."

"It's true, you helped me a lot, except that the doctor died suddenly and we had to abandon the case."

"Take it easy. I don't want any money."

"No?"

"No."

"Then what do you want?"

She let the conversation fall into an unsettling silence. Then she finally said: "I want to finish the chat we started."

"What chat?" I was affecting an unconvincing naïveté.

"The kiss you gave me."

"What about the kiss?"

"I want to go on with it. That's how you can pay what you owe me."

That was what I was afraid of. Not that Fatima wasn't an attractive woman, and the fact that she was a prostitute did spice the promise of an adventure with tantalizing flavors. But it was a matter of timing; I felt a commitment to Beatriz that I myself couldn't explain. In any case, if I tried explaining it to someone, that someone wouldn't be Fatima. I didn't want to wound her self-esteem, and she actually had helped me at a moment in the investigation when all I'd discovered up to then was that women were an illusion.

And besides that, she had initiated that kiss. Why the hell did I kiss her, in the taxi, when we'd already said goodbye? And since when did the way I kiss become irresistible? No good blaming it on alcohol. My ex-wife would say claiming alcohol was responsible was "very simplistic."

Could it be that at last a prostitute was reacting favorably to my affection, unlike that first experience at the brothel when I was an adolescent and spent my twenty minutes sitting in a chair, trying in vain to get an erection?

The voice of Tulio Bellini once again echoed in my head with one of his lapidary phrases: *The man of integrity accepts the consequences of his acts, whether good or bad.*

After the two seconds this reflection took, I asked Fatima: "What are you doing right now?"

"Nothing." I noted a tinge of victory in her voice.

"Then come on over."

I confess to having felt a little anxious about the decision. Not so much because of Beatriz, to whom in reality I had no commitment, nor myself, well accustomed to my own conflicts, but because of a reversal of values I felt taking place. In the final analysis, who was the prostitute—Fatima or me? Who would be paying whom? And paying what?

As I always did when issues became too numerous, I poured myself a generous glass of Jack Daniel's and played Robert Johnson at full volume. To me, listening to him was like consulting an oracle. His voice took me back to the bookcase in Tulio Bellini's office. More precisely, to the old *Dictionary of Classical Mythology.* To be exact, Robert Johnson's voice took me back to line 51 of the entry for *Rômulo.*

6

RÔMULO *(Romulus). Romulus and Remus were saved*

TONY BELLOTTO ◆ 119

*by a she-wolf who had just given birth and took pity
on the two children. By suckling them, she prevented
their starving to death. It is known that the she-wolf
is an animal consecrated to the Roman god Mars, and
it is widely believed that that the wolf was sent by the
god to care for the children. In addition, a woodpecker
(Mars's bird) helped the wolf feed them. Soon the shep-
herd Faustulus appeared and encountered the children
fed in this extraordinary manner. Taking pity on them,
he delivered them to his wife, Acca Larentia, who
raised them. Some skeptical mythologists, supported
especially by Church fathers, contend that the she-wolf
was none other than Acca Larentia herself, whose bad
behavior earned her the surname Lupa (Latin for she-
wolf), the term designating prostitutes.*

While Robert Johnson was singing "Me and the
Devil Blues," the lonely old lady next door banged on
the wall several times to complain about the noise,
but the only sound that made me turn down the volume was the ringing of the doorbell.

It was Fatima.

I could try recounting here how the events unfolded
until the consummation of our sexual relationship.
All that ritual that any adult human being knows and
that, despite one or another variation, always com-

prises the same thing: kisses, sucking, hair, friction, penetration, saliva, secretion, ejaculation, spasms, and mixed odors of flowers and urine.

I would like to be able to narrate exactly how the lay took place, but my active and intense involvement in the process prevents me from describing it in detail.

Let's just say that I remember very well even today her breath hot from a cigarette and the humid texture of her tongue. And the size and opulence of her breasts, to me always the most pleasurable part of the female body. And also the enveloping fragrance, both alluring and repelling, of her vagina, as well as its feverish temperature.

What I can state with certainty is that after my drive exhausted itself in a prolonged orgasm, I was overcome by the desire for her to leave immediately. That desire was suffused with a sense of guilt, as if unconsciously I wanted to blame myself for betraying Beatriz, when in reality I was to blame for betraying myself. But these thoughts didn't last long; after all, it was just sex, I thought, and *a good professional is always a good professional*, as Dora Lobo would say.

So I put a full stop on my digressions of conscience and invited Fatima to have something to eat at the August Moon. My thought was that it would be easier to get rid of her there with the excuse that my mother was coming to visit me in the morning, making it impossible for her to spend the night with me.

We sat at the table I usually occupied, and Antonio winked at me in a gesture of male bonding, something he always did when he saw me in the company of a woman.

We almost didn't talk during the meal, but over coffee I asked Fatima if she knew Miguel or Manuel, the foreigner Dora had mentioned in our conversation in the office that afternoon.

"He's a Chilean scumbag. His name is Miguel. He performs in sex shows and sleeps with men and women for money."

Later, reviewing the events of the night before I went to sleep, I remembered that during our "settling of accounts" (i.e., sexual relations) the phone rang insistently, twice in a row. Though I was occupied with Fatima, I still felt some tugs at my heart thinking about the probable caller.

I was in love with Beatriz. I was in the habit of falling in love with the wrong woman.

MAY 25

Friday

1

Pompilio Nagra, despite his name calling to mind an elderly person, was young, athletic, and well dressed. Vigorous, he moved with decisive strides and seemed always to be in motion even when standing still. This was the man I was supposed to shadow.

His overall appearance was that of an odious yuppie, a type very much in style those days, characterized by cultivated egoism and excessive preoccupation with his bank account and the perfect working of his own body.

The following morning I trailed him, enough to allow me to formulate a complete dossier of his methodical and predictable personality.

At seven a.m. he jogged for forty minutes, and then ensconced himself in a fitness center for an hour. From there, he emerged elegantly dressed and headed to an organic-food luncheonette where he consumed a perfectly balanced breakfast of vitamins and nutrients meeting the daily needs of his system. One detail: he drank only mineral water.

Afterward, he went to his place of work and remained there until lunchtime.

At two p.m., Pompilio and our client Fabian Fegri (his partner and for practical purposes his double, since Fabian was also a well-dressed yuppie, successful, and the type who has his nails done by a manicurist) left the building housing their office and walked to a restaurant on Avenida São Luís, conversing in a lively fashion.

The restaurant was located on the ground floor of a luxury hotel that, because of its proximity to the Itália Building, was familiar to all in Dora's office (it wasn't unusual for us to have lunch there with clients from time to time).

Since my job was to follow Pompilio at Fabian's order, I saw no problem in stepping out until the lunch finished, given the impossibility of one betraying the other while they ate.

Before leaving, I arranged with Eusebio, the maître d', to call me at the office as soon as they asked for the check.

I went to Dora's den to find out the latest.

2

For a few hours I had completely forgotten the death of Rafidjian, but it was impossible not to remember it when I entered the office and saw Rita clipping newspaper items that mentioned the crime.

Noticing my inquisitive gaze, she explained: "Dora wants to put together a file with all the reports on the Rafidjian case."

"What for? She told me she didn't want anything more to do with the crime."

"Bellini . . ." Rita looked at me as if to say, *Don't you know what Dora's like?*

I glanced at the clippings. Nothing new. I asked, "Any messages for me?"

"Two. Iório called very early to let you know he and Detective Boris are meeting tonight at the Bisteca d'Ouro. He'd like you to be there at one a.m. And then Beatriz rang." Rita gave me a loaded smile. "She asked you to call her back."

"When?"

"When you got in."

"No, when did she call, Rita?"

"Just now . . . fifteen minutes ago. Want me to place the call for you?"

"No thanks." It was better to make the call without Rita's meddlesome presence. "I'm going back to my post. If Eusebio calls, tell him I'm on my way and let me know."

I went to open the door to Dora's private office to say hello, but an intricate violin solo made me change my mind.

3

On the way back to the restaurant where my yuppies were having lunch, I stopped at a pay phone.

"Hello? Is Beatriz in?"

"Speaking."

"Beatriz?"

"Bellini?"

"I've been thinking about you."

"Is that good?"

"It's at least a little disturbing," I replied.

"Did you call me yesterday?" she asked.

"Yes, but you weren't home. I think I spoke with your mother."

"Yes, you did. I called back when I returned, but you weren't in either."

"Yeah, I went out." I felt a twinge of guilt in my chest. "Want to have dinner with me?"

"Today?"

"Today doesn't work. I've got a meeting with Boris and another cop."

"The Rafidjian case?" she asked.

"They must want to check some information."

"I've been following the news in the papers. I didn't know your name is Remo. I like Remo."

"You like it?" I felt confused, naked. "I hate it. So then, dinner tomorrow?"

"What time? I've got plans early in the evening."

"Plans? Forgive the directness, Beatriz, but do you have a boyfriend?"

"I like direct people. No, I don't have a boyfriend, Remo."

"Must you say *Remo* all the time?"

"I think Remo is pretty."

"I'll pick you up around midnight, but I'll call beforehand, okay? First I have a yuppie to tuck in for the night."

"A yuppie? I love yuppies."

"It's a new case we've taken on. My job is to keep tabs on a yuppie. Apropos of which, I detest yuppies. See you tomorrow."

"Till then."

Anyone looking at Pompilio Nagra and Fabian Fegri chatting amiably would never have guessed one of them had hired a detective to shadow the other.

Anyone who saw me speaking passionately on the phone with Beatriz wouldn't guess that the night before I was inside Fatima and howling like an animal.

The phantoms of my father and my ex-wife would attack me at any moment, it was just a matter of time. Trying to avoid them, I concentrated on following Pompilio, without unnecessary musing. Impossible. His routine was so boring that he couldn't even distract me.

I found absolutely no indication of his supposed betrayal. If he were a proven Judas I might even admire him a little, or at least convince myself that he was a human being full of contradictions and conflicts like anyone else. But no. Pompilio Nagra was a caricature of a productive and efficient robot.

I had to remember Dupin, Sherlock Holmes, Father Brown, Poirot, Sam Spade, the Continental Op, Nick and Nora Charles, Lew Archer, Nero Wolfe, and so many other detectives (not forgetting their spirited sidekicks like Dr. Watson and Archie Goodwin, among others) in order to convince myself I had made the right choice to give up a career in law.

At eleven thirty p.m. the lights in Pompilio's apartment went dark.

I headed home and drafted a bureaucratic report devoid of action.

I checked my watch: 12:47 a.m.

I noted that I felt excited at the prospect of seeing Boris and Iório again.

The Rafidjian case had become the focus of my attention again now that Beatriz had agreed to dinner with me the following night.

4

I entered the large, smoky space at the Bisteca d'Ouro and spotted Iório and Boris sitting at the last table on the left.

Iório was savoring the traditional fillet appetizer with slices of bread that he dipped in a sauce. He washed it down with long swallows of beer.

Boris sat motionless before an untouched glass of guarana. He seemed distant, as if still thinking about the photos of Camila and Dinéia, and I had the impression he barely recognized me when I greeted him. Iório, however, was warm and exaggerated, as was his wont, awkwardly kissing me on both cheeks the way women do when they meet.

He was the first to question me, with (I admit) quite a bit of irony in his voice: "Just what *cazzo* of a case have you gotten yourself into?"

"What *cazzo*? What case?"

"Rafidjian." Turning to Boris: "Tell him."

Boris removed his heavy glasses and cleaned them with a white handkerchief. He replaced them on his face, took a sip of guarana, lit a cigarette, and said: "Neither Camila nor Dinéia ever saw any Dr.

Rafidjian, and they don't know anyone who did."

"What do you mean?"

Boris stared at me from behind his thick lenses: "They've never heard of him and haven't the slightest idea what this is all about."

"You mean I've been following false leads?" I felt awful.

"Whatever lead you followed would have been false," replied Boris. "Rafidjian wasn't known at the Dervish. He was never there, inside or outside. He was never there, and he didn't have contact with any of the dancers."

"Are you sure?"

Iório jumped in to reply: "The police are sure."

"The police are sometimes wrong," I ventured.

"Not this time," declared Boris. "The secretary of justice is worried about the publicity surrounding the case and is demanding a quick resolution. Our investigations have led us to believe Ana Cíntia Lopes was a lie invented by the doctor."

I needed some time to process this. Iório asked the waiter for two beers and Boris took a long drag on his cigarette, while gazing into infinity through the white wall.

"If everything was an invention of Rafidjian's, how do you explain that I found two girls who correspond to Ana Cíntia's physical description and that both disappeared the month before, as he had told Dora. Coincidence?"

"It's possible," answered Boris. "He could have been a crazy mythomaniac who fell in love with the dancer just from seeing her there on the sidewalk. Then when she disappeared, he became desperate and hired a detective to find her. The problem is that the man didn't appear to be crazy, just the opposite. He was a normal doctor, a family man, a stable guy. All the statements by family and friends agree: Samuel Rafidjian Jr. was an affable man with no enemies."

"What about that name, *Ana Cíntia Lopes?*" I asked, uneasy.

"That name is meaningless," Boris replied wearily.

"If the guy was crazy," Iório said, "that was the only time in his life that he showed it. In any case, crazy or not, why was he murdered?"

We both turned to Boris, who shook his head. "I don't know. At times like this it's necessary to review the most unusual and unlikely facts. At the start of his career, Rafidjian performed a surgery, perhaps his first one, that from a certain angle could be seen as a clue, or a quasi clue. Rafidjian was thirty at the time and had just returned from the United States, after a two-year residency in pediatrics at Memorial Sloan Kettering Cancer Center. Upon his arrival he was hired by the Clinical Hospital of São Paulo, and his first surgery was on an eight-year-old boy with a brain tumor. The boy survived but became blind. His parents were really shaken, and a nurse remembers hearing the father shout in the hospital corridor: 'My son is blind! The doctor blinded my son!'"

He removed his glasses again and used the handkerchief to clean the lenses that were constantly clouding up. I noticed that without his glasses, Boris himself looked blind.

"It may seem crazy," he said, slightly embarrassed, "but the fact that Rafidjian, when he was killed, had his eyes gouged out, made me think of some kind of old vengeance. For now, we've only located the nurse, who confirmed the story; my men are checking on the others involved in the incident."

I was about to say something, but he cut me off: "Even if this hypothesis is right, we still have no explanation for why Rafidjian hired Dora Lobo to find the dancer he called Ana Cíntia . . . Ana Cíntia . . . Shit, I've drawn a blank."

"Lopes," Iório supplied.

"What about the Mafia, Abel Focca, and the Tureg brothers?" I asked.

"Frankly," Boris responded, "I haven't found the slightest link between them and Rafidjian. Like oil and water, they don't mix."

"You mean, in reality the police don't have a clue

about the crime," I concluded. "And when the press finds out, what are you going to say?"

"Don't ask me," said Boris.

"Sons of bitches," added Iório.

I desperately wanted to discover some lead, as if that would prove all my work hadn't been in vain. I asked: "What about the doctor's wife?"

"Dona Sofia?" Boris appeared more and more disheartened by the minute. "Dona Sofia thinks the police suspect her, and there's no way to change her mind. She and Rafidjian had a very formal relationship, almost like they didn't really know each other. Sofia refers to her husband as if he were some distant relative. Odd."

"But do the police have any reason to suspect her?" I asked.

He took some time to reply: "None."

5

Boris left, alleging fatigue.

I remained with Iório under the pretext of helping him finish the beer, but in reality I was trying to desensitize myself from those revelations. It was frustrating to learn that all my investigations had been useless and that at this point the case was even more mysterious than on the day of the murder.

I was anxious to hear Dora's thinking about the

new information, but it was three thirty a.m. Besides, I remembered that soon Pompilio Nagra would be waking up for his morning jog. Damn. Another night wasted on a hypothesis and digressions about a crime that didn't concern me. I left there in a hurry, despite Iório's insistence that it was still early, and glimpsed Stone accompanied by two plainclothes cops. The snitch was up to his usual routine of ratting people out, probably responding to questions with "yes," "no," and "I don't know." He saw I was watching him, and I felt like saying, *Fuck you*, but he averted his gaze and pretended not to recognize me.

The night was lost beyond redemption.

I went home, showered, shaved, made some strong coffee, and put on a Freddie King tape. Freddie, with Albert and B.B., comprise the mythological King triad, the three kings of blues. The brightness of morning invaded the room along with his voice: *"Have you ever loved a woman? So much you tremble in pain . . ."* I thought about Beatriz. I wrote a reminder to myself and pinned it with thumbtacks to the inside of the living room door: *Make reservations at Govinda.*

Some time later, I called Dora, aware I would be interrupting her aikido exercises.

She was excited by the news that Rafidjian was unknown to everyone at the Dervish. "I knew it," she said. "Didn't I tell you there was something wrong, something that didn't fit?"

"You're truly a genius, Dora."

"Don't be sarcastic, Bellini. I know it's irritating to tail a boring businessman, but what can we do? We've got to work."

Nothing like a suspicion confirmed to put Dora Lobo in an unshakable good mood.

MAY 26

Saturday

1

Govinda was an Indian restaurant where over three years ago I had proposed marriage to my ex-wife. I was in love at the time, which explains why I had good memories of the dinner.

The hypnotic twanging of the sitar, the inebriating spices of the food, and the smoothness of the wine gave the place an atmosphere conducive to revelations and confidences. My intentions became quite clear when I invited Beatriz to the same restaurant and, "if possible," as I told the guy handling reservations, the same table beside the fireplace.

Pompilio Nagra didn't disappoint me. The man was so methodical that, after an uneventful Saturday, he turned out the lights in his apartment at exactly the same time as the night before, eleven thirty. I immediately called Beatriz from the first pay phone I found. As I usually did on such occasions, I borrowed Dora's car, a new Voyage with a tape player, allowing me to pick up Beatriz to the sound of Robert Johnson, for my money the most profound and transcendental bluesman on the face of the earth.

The dinner went well, with each of us trying to show the other our best side, the best smiles, the best angles, the best and wittiest observations. All of it was by way of preparation, and to my surprise (a pleasant one) Beatriz liked as much or more than I did drinking the perfectly chilled white wine that I had ordered from the gender-ambiguous waiter.

"Do you always come here?" she asked after we had finished the meal.

"The last time, I married the woman who was with me."

"Do you get married a lot?" she said, smiling.

"Just once, and it was a disaster."

"Why?" Beatriz's question confirmed the suspicion that my marital failure made women curious.

"Because it was a rushed marriage," I replied. "We didn't know each other well, and our life together ended up proving our total incompatibility."

"Was she a lawyer like you?"

"Like *us*," I corrected.

Beatriz shook her head. "I haven't graduated yet. And I'm thinking of dropping out."

"Why?"

"Because I'm disillusioned with the law."

"I've experienced the same thing."

"Working with all of you these days has made me see how I gravitated into law school due to an illusion—"

"You think the law is an illusion?" I interrupted, thinking about Khalid.

"Huh?"

"No, nothing. Go on," I said.

"I don't think anything is an illusion. Especially law. I don't want to be a lawyer, I can't picture myself as a lawyer, I don't want to learn about the laws." She raised her glass to her lips and drank what was left of the wine. "I want to meet people."

"Preferably men?"

"Not necessarily; if I only wanted to meet men, I'd stay in law. Everyone working in the juridical system is male."

"Ah, but don't forget that justice is represented by a woman!"

"A blindfolded woman, a woman who doesn't see."

"Of course! With all those pedantic, horrible men who work in court . . ."

She smiled. "You're a really funny guy."

"No, I'm a realist."

"I think you're different."

"Different from . . . ?"

"Other men. You're frank, sincere. I have a problem with men."

I felt adrenaline coursing through my veins. A terrible suspicion overcame me: "Don't you . . . like men?"

She shook her head, laughing. "I'm not a lesbian, don't worry. I just have a hard time relating to men, that's all."

"So your problem is relationships, not men."

"No, it's with men. A specific man."

"A boyfriend? A lover?"

"Nothing like that."

"A married man? A professor?"

"Let's drop it," she said flatly. "I know you're a detective, but don't try to investigate my problems."

"I'm not here as a detective, you know that."

"Sorry, I know you're a nice guy. It was something that happened a long time ago, a man who hurt me . . . a difficult relationship, painful." I noticed tears welling in the corner of her lower eyelids. "I don't want to talk about it, okay?"

At that moment the waiter showed me the empty bottle and I asked him to bring another. Beatriz took advantage of the break to go to the bathroom.

I feared our dinner would sink into a sea of tears and white wine.

2

"You're going to give up law and do what?" I asked when she returned.

"Psychology, I think."

"Psychology has elements in common with law insofar as it involves the investigation and exposing of the truth." Wine and the intention of changing the subject had suddenly transformed me into an eloquent professor.

"Is that right?" she said, still a bit despondent.

"Besides," I continued in my alcoholic logorrhea, "the investigative method of psychoanalysis is quite close to the detective's method of investigation. I've always said that Sigmund Freud is the patron saint of detectives."

"It's true," she said, finally smiling.

I've always been lacking in the perception of romantic timing; at least that's what my ex-wife used to say. Lacking or not, I felt it was the moment to make a move.

"Beatriz, I have to tell you something."

"Go ahead."

"I can't stop thinking about you."

"Really, Remo?"

"Don't call me Remo."

"Why? I don't understand. Remo is such a pretty name; it's unique."

It was my turn to evoke the painful past. I interrupted the flow of romantic declaration to tell her the details of the premature death of my twin and my father's frustrated expectations of me, always pushing me by saying Romulo wouldn't have been such a disappointing son. And how all of it created a hatred in me for my own name. "Remo the Two-in-One! Remo the Wary! Remo the Letdown!"

Beatriz glanced around at the neighboring tables and then stared at me as if a straitjacket could solve my case. "Have you undergone analysis, Bellini?"

"No, I never thought I needed it."

"Don't take this the wrong way, but if *you* don't need it, who does?"

I felt like telling her that she would fit very well in that category, but in keeping with the upbringing my parents had given me, I swallowed my words and counterattacked with a different kind of question: "Why don't you let me solve your problem with men?"

"What you think you can solve is already solved. I don't have any problem with sex. Just the opposite, I love sex. My pain is more serious. Deeper."

That statement shut down the cycle of conversation temporarily.

After coffee, we resumed our dialogue on a less personal note. I raised the question once again of her future pursuits: "Beatriz, if you're disappointed with law and feel attracted to psychology, why not opt for a middle ground and become a detective? You've already proved you have a knack for it."

"No, I don't have a knack for lying . . . I'm not saying detectives are liars, you understand, but detectives do have to deceive, and I can't deceive."

"Forgive me for saying so," I replied, "but I must agree with Dora: lawyers also have to deceive, twist, and distort."

"I know. That's why I want to leave law school. I'm fed up with lies and now I'm looking for truth, as naive as it may sound."

"It's not naive, it's sincere. You may not believe it, Beatriz, but I'm also looking for the truth, and you know where the search has led me?"

She shook her head.

"To Dora Lobo's office. Two years ago my life collapsed like an imploding building. I didn't fit into the world. My marriage was a joke, my job was a lie, my submission to my father was idiotic, and I . . . I was an imposter."

"But not any longer." Beatriz took my hand between hers. And we kissed. I closed my eyes and felt her tongue dart across my teeth, my gums, the roof of my mouth, my tongue. I felt my dick swell, like

Lazarus rising from the tomb. I heard the crackling of wood in the fireplace beside us. The sound seemed to spring from inside my body and for a moment I imagined my heart burning red-hot like the heart of Jesus in the picture on the wall in Dinéia's house.

"Remo," she murmured.

"Just promise not to call me Remo unless we're alone . . ."

3

In the car, we listened to Robert Johnson.

"Where do you want to go?" I asked, trying to sound detached.

"Home. Tomorrow is Sunday, and I spend Sundays with my father."

"I don't like Sundays," I said.

"No one does. Not even my father, and that's why he wants his daughter with him. To numb the boredom."

"Dora told me you're planning a trip to Europe."

"Yes. My plan is to spend the July break traveling with some girlfriends."

"Do you have the money already?"

"Yes. I mean, what I lack, my father will provide. The work I did was more a matter of self-affirmation than being short of dough."

"Where are you going?"

"Home."

"No, where are you going in Europe?"

"You're very curious!"

"Curiosity is fundamental in my line of work, you know that."

"I'd like to get to know a few cities. Barcelona, Rome, Venice, and of course Paris."

"Rome. I'd like to see Rome," I said without thinking, but immediately knew it was the truth. I really did want to visit Rome.

"Oh, Remo . . . that's so obvious!" She ran her hand over my thigh. "You really should let everyone call you Remo."

"That's not what we agreed on."

"You need to meet a friend of mine, a genius psychoanalyst. It can't hurt to try, why don't you give it a shot?"

"I think I'm afraid I'll discover I'm a fool."

MAY 27
Sunday

I trailed Pompilio Nagra, and he didn't betray his partner even on Sunday. I already believed the suspicion was the fruit of Fabian Fegri's paranoia. It was common for people to become paranoid. There was paranoia about nuclear war, ecological disasters, planetary alignment, the economic crisis, terminal disease, urban violence, the prophecies of Nostradamus, earthquakes, tsunamis, and I don't know what else. Maybe Fabian Fegri needed a shrink more than a detective. Maybe *I* needed a shrink.

Perhaps Beatriz was right. Perhaps not. Who could that mysterious man she mentioned be? What "serious" and "deep" pain was it that had brought tears to her eyes? I could investigate her life without her knowing, but it wouldn't be fair. I'd never forgive myself. Better to forget her. I didn't need another complicated woman in my life.

Still, I thought of nothing but her the entire day.

It was impossible to forget her. I remembered her breasts, which I had glimpsed at the pizzeria, and the photos she took of Dinéia in Cornélio Procópio. And her murmuring, "Remo," sticking her tongue in my ear while I drove Dora's car. I remembered I didn't have a car of my own. I remembered I had screwed Fatima and hadn't given a thought to her since. I remembered that Rafidjian was dead and the police had no clue as to the killer.

Finally, I remembered that I was a detective who was wasting a Sunday shadowing Pompilio Nagra. I was starting to develop a soft spot for Pompilio. He was just another harmless lonely guy like me. I felt like abandoning my assignment and inviting Pompilio to shoot the breeze over a couple of beers. Then I picked up the Walkman and listened to Muddy Waters until the urge to open up to Pompilio went away.

We were irredeemably trapped in our solitude, that was all.

MAY 28

Monday

1

I started the day at six thirty a.m. by surveilling Pompilio's jogging.

My initial annoyance was gradually transforming into a kind of comprehension. After all, what was wrong with running every day? Wasn't it good for the health? What harm was there in wanting to preserve one's body? Was it a crime to work hard to make a lot of money? Pompilio was another victim, like me. He was lost, but who was I to judge him?

On the other hand, why had I suddenly become so understanding? Was I lightening up merely because I found myself in love with Beatriz? Was love so redeeming? Could this excess of doubts, which wasn't capable of resolution by simply downing some Jack Daniel's, be the sign that I actually did need a psychoanalyst?

Certainty a night of sex with Beatriz would solve everything.

* * *

At lunchtime, as Pompilio and Fabian sat together in the restaurant on Avenida São Luís, I went to a pay phone to call Beatriz. As I dialed, a childish feeling of pride overcame me.

I immediately broke off the connection. *What if she already called me first?* I wondered.

This puerile consideration led me to contact Dora; I phoned the office to see if Beatriz had in fact called.

Rita answered and, as soon as I identified myself, said somewhat hysterically: "Bellini, thank God! Dora keeps asking every five minutes if you've called yet."

"Why?" I asked. "She knows I'm following 'Pompous' Nagra."

"There's a new development." Rita imitated the pitch of Dora's voice: "'When he arrives, tell him to drop whatever he's doing and come to the office immediately.'"

"What's the development?"

"Come at once, something's happened."

"Shit, what—"

"If I tell you, I'll get fired. You know how she is!"

"What about Pompilio?"

In response, she pointed the mouthpiece of her phone toward Dora's office. Paganini convinced me the matter was serious.

I hung up and walked quickly toward the Itália Building.

Upon arrival, I went right up to the fourteenth floor. Rita greeted with a wordless smile, and when I entered the inner office I saw Dora standing by the window. Her expression was one of satisfaction.

She lowered the volume on the record player and, as if following a ritual, said, "Sit down." Then she served me whiskey (her glass was half full of port), lit a cigarillo, went back to the window, and began the account. "Bellini, I consider myself a lucky person. Early this morning, when I arrived at work, as soon as I came in I saw a woman of not more than forty sitting on the sofa in the anteroom. She was attractive, nicely dressed in a coffee-colored tailleur. Her face was familiar, and she looked exhausted, as if she hadn't slept for several nights. She was accompanied by a tall young man of maybe twenty. As I had no interview scheduled, I came into my office, called Rita, and asked, 'Who are they?' 'Sofia Rafidjian and her son Samuel III. She apologized for coming without an appointment, but says she urgently needs to speak with you.'"

Dora looked at me with a triumphant smile on her face. She took a puff and continued: "They came in timidly and sat down. The boy was tall like his father and remained silent throughout the conversation. He sat beside his mother, holding her hand and squeezing it from time to time when she got carried away. Sofia was eloquent and articulate, occasionally slipping into bouts of despair."

Okay, Dora, now let's get to the nitty-gritty, I thought, and she must have understood, because she then said: "Sofia apologized for coming to my office at that hour, 'on a Monday as well,' and said, 'After a weekend without sleep, I've decided to hire you, Dora, for reasons that distress me. The main one is that I don't have confidence in the police and I think they're going to end up suspecting me.'

"'What makes you think that, Sofia?' I asked. 'May I call you Sofia?'

"'Of course, Dora,' she said. 'Call me whatever you like. I think the police are going to suspect me because they're saying Samuel had lovers and hung out with prostitutes, so they're going to come around to thinking I killed him over jealousy or some such thing . . .'

"'Are you jealous, Sofia?' I asked her.

"'No, that's not the problem,' she said. 'The problem is that I never suspected my husband could betray me, and the whole story seems like a nightmare from which I can't wake up. Despite what the newspapers say, I simply can't believe Samuel was involved with prostitutes or even the Mafia, as some reports suggested. I want to hire you, Dora, to find out who killed my husband and why. By satisfying this unhappy curiosity, I also protect myself from the unfounded suspicions of the police.'

"That's what she said, Bellini, and despite the confidence I have in Boris's ability to solve the crime, I couldn't deny her rationale."

Dora was trying to appear evenhanded but she couldn't disguise the almost childish joy she felt at getting a second crack at the case.

2

Lobo laid out her plan. "First, I want you to stop working on the Pompilio Nagra case."

Immense happiness flooded over me. *I don't need any shitty psychoanalysis*, I thought.

Dora went on: "We've hired a new intern to start working today in your place. All you have to do is pass along your reports."

"A new intern? Why not Beatriz?" I asked.

"I already spoke with her. But she's disillusioned with detective work as a career, and even with the respect she feels for us, she won't be able to accept the offer."

"She's a woman with a strong personality," I concluded, like a lovesick Pierrot.

Dora pretended not to have heard me. "The

idea is very simple: we're going to investigate on two fronts. I'll interrogate here in my office, by phone or in person, all Rafidjian's family members and close friends. I want to compile a detailed profile of his personality." She was now seated at her desk, drawing geometric sketches on a sheet of paper. "You're going to hit the street looking for hidden connections in Rafidjian's life. Start by finding out what the police learned. Boris will be glad to know we're back. He and I have solved some lovely cases. Difficult, intricate, magnificent cases—"

"What makes a case magnificent?" I cut in.

"A case that can't be solved by either logic or science. A case solved almost by accident."

"Like this one, for instance?"

"Beats me!" she said. "We still haven't had time to apply logic, much less science. The data is lacking. Speaking of which, what are you waiting for? Get to work, Bellini."

So much excitement confused me.

I caught a cab to the August Moon for lunch—a succulent fillet, rare, with tomato salad and four glasses of beer on tap.

Antonio asked, "How's life going?"

"Going."

"What's with the girl you brought here the other day?"

"Who?"

"The one with the tits."

"Is that all you think about, you pervert?" I said.

"No. I think about asses too."

After an espresso I walked home to the Baronesa de Arary and put on some blues by Charley Patton. I was getting mentally organized. I would need to find some people again, and Fatima came to mind. Why were boobs and asses so obsessively fascinating? I thought about Camila and Dinéia. Digestive languor was beckoning me to go to sleep, but I resisted for a moment. I phoned Boris, setting up a meeting for the end of the afternoon.

Then I slept and don't remember dreaming.

3

"José Maria Arcoverde, that's the name."

I had been sleeping, the phone rang, I answered, and the voice at the other end uttered that unfamiliar name.

"Nobody here by that name. Wrong number."

"José Maria . . . Don't hang up, Remo. It's me."

"Beatriz?"

"Uh-huh."

"Who is José Maria Arcoverde?" I asked, awake now. "The man who hurt you?"

"Forget that. I was drunk that night. Don't believe everything a woman tells you."

"When they're drunk I believe them," I said. "Who is José Maria Arcoverde?"

"Your future psychoanalyst. I already spoke to him. He's waiting for you to call him. Write down the phone number and the address of his office."

"Hold on, Beatriz. I was sleeping."

"Sleeping? At seven p.m.?"

"Seven? Christ, I've gotta find Boris!"

"See? If I hadn't called, you'd miss your appointment."

"Can we talk about the psychoanalyst some other time?" I got out of bed with the phone tucked between ear and shoulder.

"Do this," she said, "and we'll have dinner. But I choose the restaurant, okay?"

"Okay."

"Do you like Japanese food?"

"If it's with you, I like any kind of food."

I know, it was a second-rate attempt at flirtation. I've had that problem since childhood. We hung up.

I called Boris to tell him I was running late. Since his shift was ending, he asked me to meet him in an hour at the Bisteca d'Ouro.

I showered, gathered up some reports, and hailed a cab on Avenida Paulista.

4

When I showed up, Boris was seated at the table usually occupied by Iório. He was alone.

I said: "Sorry about the delay, I was finalizing a few reports and lost track of the time."

"No problem, I still don't have any clues."

"What about the blind boy?" I asked, taking a seat.

"The blind boy is now twenty-six, married, and lives in the United States. In Miami, to be exact. His name is Pedro Paulo Xavier."

"And his father?"

"He died five years ago in a plane crash. The mother lives with Pedro Paulo and two other children in Miami." Boris smiled for the first time since I met him. "An excellent alibi, don't you agree?"

I nodded. "That aside, what's the status of the investigations?" I asked.

"Square one." He took a gulp of guarana. "Want a beer?" I said yes and he flagged down the waiter before continuing. "Here's the situation: Camila Garcia and Dinéia Duarte Isidoro had never heard of a Dr. Rafidjian or anybody fitting his description. By the way, Camila and Dinéia are definitely two different people. Camila's a junkie and is constantly wasted. The other one's a bit more shameless, but sometimes she seems like a naive little girl from the interior. Some prostitutes have very interesting personalities, Bellini."

After a short pause, he went on: "And it wasn't only them who had never heard of the doctor. Nobody who works for the nightclubs within a radius of a kilometer of the Dervish knew him. On the other hand, the man was held in high esteem by everyone who had dealings with him, from friends dating back to medical school days to recent casual acquaintances. According to Ivan Boudeni, the famous surgeon, Rafidjian was his best student. 'Samuel combined natural talent with a Spartan sense of discipline,' he told me. A man with an impeccable past, loved and admired by all—that's his reputation . . . The revenge theory has been discarded. Pedro Paulo, the blind boy, like I said, has been living in Miami with his widowed mother and sisters for many years. None of them have been in Brazil recently; I checked with the federal police. Beyond that . . . beyond that, what else? There's no evidence that Rafidjian ever committed medical malpractice. He was a calm, reserved guy. Didn't gamble or drink, not even socially. He wasn't a man with a lot of ambition, and he spent less money than he earned. A good son, good friend, good husband, good father, good doctor . . ."

"What about the autopsy?" I asked.

"The autopsy came up with some interesting data. First point: Rafidjian died from a cerebral concussion followed by acute anemia brought on by loss of blood through the eye cavities. The medical examiner thinks the killer rammed Rafidjian's head repeatedly against the corner of his desk. The part most affected was the base of the skull, which was struck with great force. After that, already unconscious but perhaps still alive, Rafidjian was shoved into the middle of the room and only then was his face lacerated and his eyes poked out with the umbrella. That's what caused the heavy loss of blood. Second point: from studying the position of the furniture and the body, the ME believes there was no resistance or struggle on the part of the victim, which seems very strange. Final point: the murderer, because they concluded that the individual acted alone, is someone relatively strong but not necessarily *very* strong. Despite the blows having required a significant amount of physical energy, the moving of the body, which was dragged to the middle of the room, apparently didn't demand much force on the part of the killer; as I said, the victim didn't resist."

"Then it's possible to draw an approximate physical profile of the murderer?"

"Yes," Boris said with a hint of sarcasm, "any

man of medium height or any reasonably strong woman—"

"Which would eliminate some of the possible suspects," I parried.

"What suspects? I don't have *any* suspects." The sarcasm in his voice had given way to irritation.

"Rafidjian's secretary, Dona Glaucia, for example."

"Why do you keep insisting on Dona Glaucia? Forget it, Bellini."

Boris lit a cigarette and fell into a pensive silence. I consulted my reports, quickly running my eyes over the typed sheets in search of something that had escaped our previous examination. Nothing. I asked Boris what he planned to do next.

"Go on looking. This is a job of patience, you've got to stay calm. At a given moment we'll discover a person or a fact that'll lead us to the killer. It's just a matter of time."

I ordered another beer.

Boris blew cigarette smoke at the ceiling and said: "I'm glad that you're all back on the case. Dora has magnificent intuition and I sometimes wonder why we don't have women like her working as police."

"The low pay, maybe?"

"What does she think about the crime?" he asked curtly.

"She doesn't go out on a limb with unsubstantiated hunches," I answered. "But she doesn't believe Rafidjian was just a voyeur in love with a hooker from the Dervish."

"Of course."

"Why of course?"

"Because he was murdered."

5

Afterward, telling me he was tired, Boris said good night.

I followed him with my eyes as he stepped outside just as Stone was coming in. Stone, limping, headed right to the bar. Seeing the informer gave me a hunch and I immediately ran out after Boris. I caught him on the sidewalk of Rua da Consolação heading toward the bus stop. There were pedestrians everywhere and the noise of traffic was deafening. I tugged at his arm.

"I just remembered something."

"What?" Boris asked, turning around.

"In one of our conversations Dora told me about a guy Stone mentioned in a statement. A foreigner called Miguel, Camila's partner in a live sex show. Later, Fatima confirmed that he's a rent boy."

I watched Boris's tiny eyes behind the thick glasses.

"Yes?" He seemed to be waiting for something more.

"That's all. I thought it might be a lead, since we don't have any others."

"It's possible," he said, taking a notepad from the inside pocket of his coat, where he jotted down the name *Miguel*. "Who did you say spoke about Miguel?"

"Stone. He's inside, right now." I pointed back toward the Bisteca d'Ouro.

He wrote down *Stone* and said: "Correct. Tomorrow I'll talk to Iório."

"Why not speak to Stone now? He just went inside," I pressed.

"I'd rather talk to Iório before having a conversation with Stone. Good night, Bellini." He turned and walked to the bus stop.

I decided not to miss the opportunity. Returning to my table, I looked for Stone. He was sitting by the counter now, like when I first saw him. I approached.

"Can I buy you a beer?" I asked cordially.

"No."

"Take it easy, I just want to ask one question."

"I don't owe you nothing, and I only talk when I owe something, okay?"

Silence.

"Get the hell outta here!" he yelled. "Get lost!"

I went back to my table and understood why Boris preferred to consult with his boss Iório before interrogating Stone.

After all, eighteen years on the force counts for something.

6

I called Dora at midnight and related the conversation with Boris. Her orders: "Find this Miguel right now."

"Now? Where?"

"How should I know? Go look for Fatima. Hustle!"

Dora could be a pain sometimes. I couldn't exactly say that I didn't want to meet Fatima because after we'd had sex, I'd immediately had the cruel desire to get her out of there as soon as possible, as if I were ashamed of her, and for that simple reason meeting with her now would be totally awkward for me. My relationship with Dora was based on complete sincerity, but there were still certain things I really couldn't tell her. She would never forgive me for snorting cocaine with Duilio or starting a sexual relationship with Fatima. If there was one thing that irritated her most, it was unnecessary intimacy with people who were aiding an investigation.

Then, since I had no desire to hear the voices of my father and my ex-wife, especially when I had a psychoanalyst waiting for my call (and who, as if that weren't enough, had an ambiguous and symbolic name, José Maria), I agreed: "Fine, Dora. I'm off on the trail. Call you tomorrow."

There were times when I felt like a real asshole.

7

I went back to the Dervish.

The letter V was burned out on the neon sign at the entrance, and so it read *Der ish*. I couldn't remember if that defect had already existed the first time I was there. A bouncer smiled at me and hookers surrounded the door.

Inside, everything seemed the same. But I didn't see Khalid (a man I was suddenly anxious to speak to) or Fatima. I walked over to the bar, greeted the vacant-eyed barista, and ordered a beer.

I asked: "Is Khalid around?"

"He's in a meeting in his office."

"Office?"

"Yeah. The office is in the rear. He'll be back soon."

Three beers later, Khalid Tureg sat down beside me, exuding his outlaw charisma (and the smell of his Bahian cigar).

"Detective! Don't tell me you're still looking for that dancer?"

"No. I found out that dancers are an illusion."

"Very good, ha ha. That makes Khalid happy."

"Now I'm looking for a man."

"A man?"

"Yeah. A foreigner named Miguel. You know him?"

"Sure I do. But he hasn't been around for some time."

"Why did he disappear?"

Khalid sucked on his cigar. "I don't know."

"What's he like?"

"Quiet and scary-looking. Always by himself."

"Physical appearance?"

"Muscular. With the face of an Indian. He doesn't like it, but the people here call him Indian. Not in front of him, of course."

"And do you know where he lives, whether he has friends, that sort of thing?"

"Ah, detective questions, eh? Ha ha . . . No, I don't . . . I don't know anything. Just that he's a very mysterious guy."

"Khalid, do you believe men are an illusion too?"

"Men? No, detective. If they were, we'd all be queer."

"Why?"

"Because the best part of life is the illusions, ha ha ha ha ha, right?"

* * *

After the Dervish, where I always learned something useless from Khalid, I walked to the Hotel Mênfis, a by-the-hour establishment on Rua Frei Caneca, and didn't find Fatima there either. I asked the desk clerk if she'd be back soon.

"Maybe yes, maybe no," he replied.

That irritated me, and I decided to go home. First, however, I left an urgent message asking her to call me.

In bed, listening to Howlin' Wolf, I thought about sushi and sashimi.

Mentally, I associated labia with tuna sashimi. I wondered whether Beatriz's labia had the texture of tuna sashimi. It would be interesting to resolve that question the following night after dinner.

I fell asleep thinking thoughts like that, but I didn't dream about Japanese food or female genitalia. I dreamed I was on Avenida Paulista at night, behind a naked girl roughly twelve years old. I only saw her from the back, some distance away. Around Trianon Park I drew closer and stared at her very pale white skin. I touched her shoulder, and when she turned her head I woke up from fright. Her eyes were completely white, without pupils.

She had smiled and said: "I'm blind."

MAY 29

Tuesday

1

The phone rang; it was Fatima.

"Bel, were you looking for me yesterday?"

"Bel? What's this *Bel?*"

"It's an affectionate nickname. *Bellini* is too formal, it sounds like the name of a lawyer. *Bel* suits you better."

"I see. I need your help, Fatima—"

"I've got some news," she said, cutting me off. "A friend, Lucila, told me she met Rafidjian. But the police don't know it yet. Lucila hates cops."

"Makes two of us. How'd she know Rafidjian?"

"It's not that she knew him; she only saw him once. It was a night when she was arriving for work at the Dervish. She saw a tall, thin man standing beside the front door. As Lucila was about to go in, the man asked, 'Do you know who Ana Cíntia Lopes is?' She said no and noticed that the man seemed very nervous and ill at ease. He said: 'You don't? She's the one who got married recently.' Lucila said, 'Married? Somebody got married?' The guy became even more uncomfortable. He was so nervous that he shoved some cash into her hand and then ran off. It wasn't till later, when the photo came out in the newspapers, that Lucila made the connection. That tall, thin guy was Rafidjian."

"And will this Lucila agree to talk with me?"

"No. No way, Bel."

My God, why did I have to put up with this? A woman calling me Bel.

"But I'm not the police, Fatima."

"To her, it's all the same thing. Police, detective, lawyer, judge, jailer."

"Why is she so suspicious?"

"Lucila's been arrested a bunch of times and has learned that those guys are all the same. They shit on whoever's there, fucked, rotting in a cell."

"But did you explain to your friend that it's a homicide and withholding evidence is a crime?"

"Nobody needs to explain that to her, Bellini; Lucila already knows it. She told me that secret because she trusts me, and I told you because I trust you. If you intend to turn my friend in to the police, it'd be better for you to never speak to me again."

"I'm not turning in anybody. I just want to make sure the information is reliable."

"Of course it is. Lucila is my friend, my sister. She wouldn't make this up."

"Fine. Thank you for alerting me. I think I owe you another one now."

How can you say something like that, Bellini? I asked myself.

"What else you wanna know?" she asked, bringing my attention back to the phone call.

"I'd like more information about that foreigner, Miguel."

"I don't know hardly anything. I know he's called Miguel and that nobody much likes him, despite his good looks."

"Did you know that people call him the Indian?"

"No, but he does have the features of an Indian."

"Do me a favor, Fatima: try to find out everything you can about him. It's very important."

"I'll try. Say, what about your mother?"

"What about her?"

"That day we . . . fucked, you told me to leave because your mother was coming the next day."

"Sure, I remember."

"Well, I want to know how your mother is."

"Dona Livia? She's doing great." *I think she's doing great* would have been more truthful, since I hadn't spoken with my mother for several months.

"Livia. A cool name." Fatima took on a sensual

tone: "Bel, I'd like to see you again."

I said: "You will, we'll go out one of these days. The problem is, right now I'm loaded down with work." Suddenly, a Machiavellian inspiration: "Do this for me, Fatima: find out something about Miguel, then call me and I'll find a way for us to get together."

After we said goodbye, I hung up the phone and heard my inner voice saying: *You bastard! You're getting used to this game.*

Then, my father's voice: *A man's integrity is measured by his capacity to shun corruption.*

Poor Tulio Bellini, I thought, and wondered where he went wrong.

2

I took a cold shower, shaved. The telephone rang again. Beatriz.

"Did I wake you up, Remo?"

"No. I just took a shower."

"I made a reservation for us at a Japanese restaurant," she said.

I thought about tuna sashimi.

"What about Zé Maria?" she asked.

Dora had a theory that women were sharper mentally than men, and she was probably right, because I didn't recall any Zé Maria, except an old-time player for the Corinthians team, but that couldn't be who Beatriz was referring to.

"Which Zé Maria?" I asked.

"The psychoanalyst, José Maria Arcoverde. His nickname is Zé Maria."

"Oh. What about him?"

"Nothing. I just wanted to know if you've been to see him."

"Not yet. You didn't give me his phone number or an address."

"Write it down!" she said, or rather, ordered.

"Beatriz, do you really think I need a shrink?"

"Of course. Psychoanalysis is a wonderful thing, it ought to be compulsory. I know a lot of psychoanalysts. I've been in therapy since childhood."

I felt sorry for her. Then a thought occurred to me: "The man who . . . hurt you. Was he by any chance a psychoanalyst?"

"Why does that matter so much to you? Solve your own problems before worrying about mine."

"Forgive me, I thought that you might have been the victim of a sick psychoanalyst, that's all. Besides, by solving your problems maybe I can solve some of my own as well."

"That has nothing to do with anything . . . I see now that you can't help me. No one can. And anyway, I don't want help! Who told you I want help? All I wanted was to recommend a psychoanalyst to you."

"Take it easy, Beatriz. I'm very glad you worry about me. I was flattered when you suggested I go to a psychoanalyst named José Maria Arcoverde." After venturing a brief pause, reflective and slightly dramatic, I continued: "José Maria. The name gives me the impression of a balanced, self-assured guy. And Arcoverde is a poetic name that suggests several interpretations. Think about Cardinal Arcoverde Street, for example. Just who was Cardinal Arcoverde? Could he perhaps be related to José Maria? I think about that kind of thing a lot. The problem is that I don't have any time right now, a homicide takes up a big space in a detective's life. I don't have time for anything, including eating and sleeping. A clue may turn up at any moment, and I have to be ready. Clues don't give advance notice of when they're going to appear, you know."

"A nice turn of phrase, Remo. Pure Dora Lobo."

I ignored the observation and its dollop of sarcasm.

"I can't start analysis before this case is solved," I went on. "Before too long I'll catch a banal adultery case or have to tail some idiot like Pompilio Nagra, then it'll be easier to go into analysis. And English too; I want to take an English-language course. Would you be willing to give me Zé Maria's address after we finish the Rafidjian case?"

"No, that's fine. I like you the way you are, kind of neurotic."

"What do you mean, *kind of neurotic*?"

"You know, Remo, that business of saying you hate your own name. That's kind of neurotic."

"We'll talk tonight," I said. "What time do you want me to come for you?"

"Is nine all right?"

"Agreed."

I jotted down a reminder and thumbtacked it beside the door: *Ask to borrow Dora's car. Pick up Beatriz at nine. Tuna sashimi.* I underlined that last phrase.

3

Later, for the third time that morning, the telephone: "Bellini?"

"Dora?"

"Be at the office at 1 o'clock sharp."

I looked at my watch: 12:15.

"What's going on?" I asked.

"Stone, Iório's informant, has a revelation to make. He called me this morning." Dora proceeded to relate the conversation word for word:

"'Detective Lobo?'

"'Speaking.'

"'You're a woman? That's funny. I thought Detective Lobo was a man.'"

"He's annoying," I said.

"He has the unpleasant habit of using English words in the middle of sentences. I actually found him slightly amusing," she said. "He wanted to sell me information that, according to him, would turn the case upside down. Early this morning Boris called him to get him to make a statement at homicide about the murder of Rafidjian. Except he couldn't go to the precinct for fear of his role as informant being discovered by criminals and dirty cops. So Boris suggested they meet at the Bisteca d'Ouro and Stone proposed the following:

"'You pay me, Detective Lobo, and you can be here for my statement at the Bisteca d'Ouro. It goes without saying that Boris can't find out about the arrangement. If he does, I'll deny everything, understand?'

"'What's your reason for wanting me to be there?'

"'My information is very valuable, but the police won't be able to pay me for it. Since I know you're interested too, I won't spill it till I get money in my pocket, okay?'"

"He's a rat," I said. "What did you tell him?"

"To begin with, I negotiated a reasonable price with him—he obviously wanted to be paid in dollars, and I agreed, provided he lived up to the conditions I stipulated."

"What conditions?"

"Well, I'm curious to find out what's going on so I insisted on being there for the statement. I told Stone to find a way to move the meeting to my office, since I'm too old and too impatient to get to the Bisteca. In fact—Bellini, I no longer feel like going anywhere, with the exception of Paris or Buenos Aires from time to time."

"I don't blame you," I said.

"Besides which, I'm paying for the information, which gives me the right to choose the venue. Stone asked me for ten minutes to settle things by phone, then called back to confirm the meeting for one o'clock, here in the office, with Boris and Iório present. Of course, Stone will get here half an hour early to pocket his dollars, but that's off the books."

"How much is the son of a bitch getting?" I asked.

"No more than Sofia Rafidjian is paying me for a day's work."

"And Boris doesn't know about the arrangement?"

"Not a word," Dora replied.

"He's not going to find it suspicious that Stone wants to make a statement in your office?"

"No. Stone claimed the Bisteca would be full of cops with ties to a gang of car thieves, which would hamper his statement there, as he wouldn't want to run the risk of being recognized as an informant.

Stone didn't even need to suggest our office, Boris himself did so."

"A perfect crime."

"Not entirely. What persuaded me to do business with that scoundrel was a feeling that the information he has is extremely *hot*, as he would put it."

"I also have some *hot* information for you, so how 'bout we discuss the price?"

"You're paid by the month for that, sonny boy. What's it about?"

I related my discoveries about the foreigner Miguel the Indian, and Lucila, Fatima's friend who had seen Rafidjian.

"We need to interrogate this Lucila," she said.

"No way. She adamantly refuses to talk to police or anyone else. But according to Fatima, the information is valid."

Dora fell silent. Then she said: "That kills the theory that Rafidjian made up the whole story. He really was looking for Ana Cíntia Lopes . . . whoever Ana Cíntia Lopes is."

We hung up, and I went for a quick breakfast at the August Moon.

Antonio: "How are things?"

"A bit complicated, but quite stimulating. What about the tasses?" I asked.

"Tasses?"

"Tits and asses," I explained.

He smiled in macho complicity. "Less complicated, more stimulating."

Men by themselves can become extremely un-pleasant.

At 12:50 I caught a taxi to the Itália Building.

4

Dora was sitting at her desk. In front of her, in the chair I usually occupied, Stone. Beside the desk, manning the typewriter, a police scribe. Behind him, standing and smoking a cigarette, Boris. Leaning against the window behind Dora, Iório and me.

Stone, hyped by the audience and the money, be-gan his garrulous statement: "Look, when you asked me who Ana Cíntia, Dr. Rafidjian, and I-don't-know-who-else was, I confess I didn't have the slightest idea *who the fuck you were talkin' about*."

"Stone!" shouted Iório. "If you say one more word in English, I'll bust your skull, you shitty little dealer."

"Okay, okay. You don't need to yell," replied Stone, clearly a bit frightened. "What's gotta be made clear is that I don't read newspapers or watch TV, that's why I never noticed what that doctor guy looked like."

"Get to the point, Stone," said Iório, now calmed

by Boris, who was patting him on the shoulder.

Stone, fingering the silver ring he sported on his left ear, said: "This morning Detective Boris called me and said he wanted to hear my statement on the Rafidjian affair. After he hung up I asked somebody, 'What the fuck is the Rafidjian affair?'

"He said, 'It's that doctor who was murdered using an umbrella.'

"'An umbrella?' I said, and we both laughed.

"Then he handed me the paper he was reading. 'Take a look at the sucker here.'"

Stone made a studied, dramatic pause. He looked me in the eye, I don't know why, and continued: "When I saw the photo in the paper, I shouted: 'Shit, I know that guy!'" Stone widened his eyes and said nothing, looking at each of us in turn.

"Speak!" Iório growled.

"Well, that Dr. Rafidjian was a fag I knew from Dante Alighieri."

The vicinity of the Dante Alighieri School, in the Jardins district, transformed at night into a haunt for male prostitutes. I knew this very well, by the way, because Dante Alighieri is two blocks away from Baronesa de Arary.

"Rafidjian was gay?" asked Iório, flabbergasted.

"Yeah," Stone answered.

"That's it? That's your big revelation?" bellowed

Dora from force of habit, trying to get her money's worth.

"Take it easy," Stone replied. Iório lunged at him but Boris held him back. "There's more."

"What else?" asked Boris.

"I remember," Stone said, "that the doctor was a tall, thin guy who passed by there all the time in a metallic-blue Monza. You know how it works at Dante Alighieri: the rich faggots cruise the block in their cars and the rent boys stand on the sidewalk offering themselves to the johns. The doctor, who drew attention because he was so tall and thin, was always hugging and kissing a foreign guy named something like Manuel."

We all exchanged glances. Boris intervened: "Wait a minute. Are you sure of what you're saying?"

"Absolutely."

Boris immediately phoned homicide and ordered an APB on a foreigner called Miguel (thanks to me he knew the correct name) as a suspect in a murder. He also told them to be ready because he would return to the precinct soon with a guy to help make an artist's rendering of the suspect. "Find the artist!" he shouted. After hanging up, he addressed Stone: "Go on, please."

"That's all, folks."

"That's all, my ass," said Iório. "Tell the whole story."

"What whole story?" asked Stone.

"Well," Boris offered, "was Miguel a rent boy?"

"Yes, but from time to time he would disappear. He wasn't very consistent, just like I'm not. I only resort to it when the cash runs out."

"And you knew him?" Dora asked.

"Just by sight. I never spoke to the guy. He was standoffish and had a nasty look about him."

"But you knew him from live sex shows, didn't you?" I ventured.

"Yeah, but again, only by sight. I never shot the shit with him."

"Have you seen the guy lately?" Boris asked.

"No. That's what I was going to say. The gringo's been out of sight for a helluva long time. So, this morning when I remembered the whole story, I asked the dude who showed me Rafidjian's picture in the paper: 'Where'd the gringo go?' And he said: 'The Indian? Beats me, seems he got married and then disappeared.'"

"Married who?" Dora asked, voicing the question we all had in mind.

"I don't know, my dear."

"You son of a bitch!" Iório broke free from Boris and launched himself at Stone. Boris and I tried to restrain him, but he kept struggling, overcome with rage, while the scribe pushed Stone, limping, to the other side of the room.

Dora stood up and shouted: "Gentlemen! Please!"

Iório, once again immobilized by Boris, said, "Sorry, Dora, it's just that this son of a bitch could have let me know before. Now I'm the one to blame, 'cause he's my informant."

"Calm down, Iório," said Boris. "Stone has to go to the precinct for the sketch. We can teach him a thing or two there . . ."

In a matter of hours the foreigner Miguel was being hunted throughout the city. And despite the dollars Stone had in his pocket, I wouldn't have traded places with him.

5

Dora lit a Tiparillo and went to the window. She pushed against one of the jalousies to let in air, and this seemed to clear the room of Stone's sinister presence.

We were alone, she and I, digesting the new facts and their possible consequences.

"Now this . . . Don Quixote was gay. Amazing," said Dora.

"Do you believe it?" I asked.

"Why not?" She smiled. "I paid for it!"

She poured herself whiskey and asked if I'd like mine with or without ice. I hesitated for a few seconds, but concluded the situation demanded the drink neat.

After a generous gulp (hers was with ice), Dora took a deep drag of her cigarette and said, "If Rafidjian was gay, why was he looking for a dancer?"

"Maybe Miguel and Ana Cíntia are the same person?"

"A transvestite?" she countered. It was always a pleasant surprise when Dora took one of my theories seriously. I felt it vindicated my calling as detective.

"Why not?" I answered. "Although then we would have no explanation for the statement by Lucila, Fatima's friend, that she heard from Rafidjian that Ana Cíntia Lopes had gotten married."

"Cross-dressers get married too, Bellini. And perhaps that makes sense if added to another statement, the one by Stone's friend."

"What did he say?" I asked.

"Weren't you listening? Focus, Bellini. He said Miguel the Indian disappeared because he'd gotten married."

"If that theory is correct, it'll be hard to find out whether he married a man or a woman," I said. "What do you think about all this?"

"Nothing, as long as the gringo's still in the wind." She regarded me with shining eyes. "And why are you standing there instead of looking for

Miguel? Am I paying you to keep drinking and asking me questions?"

"One last question."

"What?"

"Can you lend me your car again tonight? I have a
dinner with Beatriz that can't be postponed."

6

We had dinner at the Hinodê restaurant, on one of
those streets decorated with Chinese lanterns. The
waitress, apparently an acquaintance of Beatriz's
(who, I imagine, frequented the establishment in
the company of her university friends), led us to a
small reserved room. We sat on the floor at a low
table, after removing our shoes, which were placed
on a shelf of dark wood. Beatriz was wearing a short
beige skirt that covered only the upper half of her
thighs, a white silk T-shirt, and a brown jacket. She
took off the jacket and dropped it onto the floor. I
saw she wasn't wearing a bra.

Since I'm not well versed in Japanese cuisine, except for sake and tuna sashimi, I let her choose the
evening's fare.

And it was precisely with tuna sashimi that we
began the meal.

"How is it you know Japanese food so well?" I
asked.

"My father is a fanatic. I've eaten in Japanese restaurants since I was a child."

"You're very precocious. From childhood on you've frequented psychoanalysts and Japanese restaurants."

"Whims of my father. He has a very strong personality. Like everyone in the family."

"I've already met your mother. On the phone. That only leaves your father."

"You don't want to meet him."

"Why not?"

"Let's just say he doesn't go out of his way to be nice to my . . . friends. Excessive possessiveness is a family trait."

"Can you believe that to this day I still don't know your family name? What's your last name?"

"Mekla," she replied, dipping a slice of tuna in a small dish of soy sauce.

"Beatriz Mekla. Are you of Arab descent?" I asked.

She nodded, chewing the fish in a scandalously sexual manner. "Lebanese."

"Lately I've been learning some things from an Arab," I said, referring to Khalid Tureg.

"We're a people of great wisdom."

"No doubt. Do you know Lebanon?"

"Quite well. My grandmother, my father's mother, still lives in Beirut. When I was small I used to spend my vacations there, and I think it's the most beautiful city in the world. Today it's hurting because of all the violence and destruction. It's been years since we went back there. Now it's my grandmother who visits us from time to time."

Beatriz ordered a plate of special sushi as entrée. I ordered more sake and continued to be impressed (I was already impressed by her choice of restaurant) by her capacity for drink.

"And what's your grandmother's name?" I inquired.

"Beatrice."

"Beatrice? And she's Lebanese?"

"It's because my great-grandfather, her father, was a professor of literature at Lebanon University. He was an expert in Italian literature, and his greatest passion was Dante's *Divine Comedy*. The name Beatrice was his way of paying homage to the book and to his daughter."

I noticed that she drank in a somewhat compulsive manner even when she seemed to be thinking about other things, her gaze hiding some morbid mystery. Maybe I was fantasizing a little, but she seemed to emanate a mixture of sex and affliction. For a moment, I felt I was in the presence of a female Edgar Allan Poe.

"A toast to Dante!" she said, pulling me from my reverie, while raising the square sake glass.

"A toast to Beatriz!" I said.

"A toast to Remo!" she said.

"A toast to Rome!" I said.

"A toast to Romulus!" she said.

"A toast to the she-wolf!" I said.

"A toast to Dora Lobo!" she said.

"A toast to Japan!" I said.

"A toast to Lebanon!" she said.

After the toasts we kissed furiously. There was a strong taste of raw fish in her mouth, which gave me an instantaneous erection. I stuck my hand in her blouse and fondled the smooth, compact mass of her breasts. Her nipples were hard and pointed upright. We were interrupted by a soft knock on the door.

The Japanese waitress smiled, said *"Onegaishimasu,"* and placed a round tray full of colored sushi on the table. She moved around the small room on her knees before leaving with a bow.

The sake opened my spirit and loosened my tongue. I told Beatriz that I had already caught a glance of her breasts when she bent down to pick up her purse at the pizzeria. She smiled, and this encouraged me to reveal other intimacies, including the resemblance I found between tuna sashimi and labia majora.

"You've really got one sick mind, Remo."

At that moment we heard whispers coming from the neighboring room. We stopped talking. We realized it was the sound of a couple making love. I said "making love," but Beatriz was more direct. She looked at me wide-eyed like a child, and declared, "They're fucking!"

We listened to the noises that increased gradually to orgasm ("They came together," Beatriz concluded), and then, suitably buzzed and turned on, we decided to imitate the couple next door. Beatriz lay down, and her skirt exposed her white panties.

I got on my knees, and she caressed herself beneath her panties while I took off my pants. She didn't undress, but the penetration happened immediately (and in an especially arousing way, since the elastic of her panties pressed against my dick the whole time). Beatriz was wet and the smell of sex mixed with the raw fish and soy sauce that covered our fingers and lips. The constant tension from the possibility of the waitress arriving at any moment created a counterpoint to the sexual rapture.

At the moment I came I shouted, "I love you!" (Later I was embarrassed when I remembered this.)

7

While we waited for the check, I told her about Stone's revelation that Rafidjian was gay, and that the prime suspect in the case was now a foreigner named Miguel, known as the Indian. I told her about my theory that perhaps Ana Cíntia and Miguel were the same person, but Beatriz didn't seem very interested. More than that, I saw my talk was boring her. That reminded me that the night still had a lot in store for me—detective work, unfortunately. I dropped her off at home to the sound of Robert Johnson, who always seemed to sing the right songs.

As I said goodbye, I mentioned that I had loved the story of her Lebanese grandmother Beatrice and I promised her a prize if she could guess where I was heading at that moment.

"I haven't the slightest idea," she replied.

"The Dante Alighieri School, to look for Miguel."

"The Dante Alighieri School," she repeated. "What synchronicity."

"Synchronicity?"

"Remo, didn't you say Freud was the greatest detective of all time? You really need to read Jung and his theory of synchronicity."

I agreed, thinking it was something like Sam Spade and Philip Marlowe. Different styles, different methods, different detectives.

8

I left the car in the garage in Dora's building and

hailed a taxi to Baronesa de Arary. I took a shower (I was sticky), changed clothes, and drank two glasses of ice water. Water was all I had in the refrigerator, and that depressed me. *Better than nothing*, I thought. I remembered how right after my separation I didn't even have a refrigerator. Just the mattress and the tape recorder. It would be worse without the recorder.

I went down Peixoto Gomide to the Dante Alighieri School, just two blocks from home. During the walk I had the impression of being followed. The same thing had happened earlier, when I stopped by the apartment before picking up Beatriz for dinner. It was a fleeting sensation that I attributed to some kind of paranoia. I even toyed with the idea that it was time to begin analysis with Zé Maria, but I soon forgot. Then, heading toward the school at night, the sensation returned. As I had done earlier, I looked behind me and saw no one. It was night, the street was empty, but the sensation wouldn't go away. I looked at Trianon Park, closed at that hour, and tried to scan the foliage behind the security bars, but the idea that someone was watching me from over there was absurd and only served to reinforce the feeling that I really did need to give Zé Maria a call.

The Dante Alighieri School was large, imposing, and traditional. It was founded by the wealthy Italian community of the city and was frequented by descendants of Italians and by children of the upper middle class who lived in the area. By one of those co-incidences that simply insist on happening, the place transformed at night into a spot for gay prostitution.

On the sidewalks surrounding the school walls, you could find youths in tight pants from the lower social classes, displaying themselves for the rich gay men who circulated in cars, sizing up the available merchandise.

I walked past there, observing the movement, but the place was lousy with plainclothes cops, which complicated my task.

Yet I had to try something.

I approached a stocky youth with pimples, wearing tight jeans and a lacy shirt. His haircut was odd, short on the sides and bushy on top. I asked him if he had a cigarette.

He looked at me with contempt and said: "What's with you, cop? I already told you guys all I know . . . Why don't you get your act together, huh? You're the third one they've sent to talk to me."

"I'm not a cop."

"Oh, then you're a customer? Or you decided to make some money and you're here to steal my spot? You must take me for an idiot if you think you can make me believe you're gay."

At that moment an older man in glasses and a mustache drove by slowly, looking at me and then at the stocky young man.

"See that?" the youth said to me. "The fag likes you, cop."

"Listen up, kid, I'm not gay and I'm not a cop. Much less a customer. But I can pay you for some information."

"Save your money. Around here we don't know much about that Miguel guy."

"Anything you know is gravy," I replied, and took out my notebook.

"In the first place"—he stood up straight and assumed a serious tone as if giving official testimony—"I'd like to make it very clear that I hate that Miguel. I didn't even know he was called Miguel; around here he was known as the Indian. I hate murderous queers. They're unprofessional and screw things up for us pros. Every so often some maniac shows up who likes to kill fags, and afterward it's us, the honest ones, who get fucked over. That guy is weird, and I only know him by sight. I know his nickname is the Indian and that he's Chilean. We once called him Argentinian and the guy got so mad he wanted to kill somebody. He said, 'I'm Chilean!' He hasn't been around here for some time. Not since before the doctor was killed."

"Do you think he killed the doctor?"

"That's what we believe."

"Why do you always say 'we'?"

"Because I'm not like that asshole Indian. I have friends and I'm part of an organized group victimized by the powerful. If we don't unite, they'll annihilate us. That's why I hate maniacs, 'cause they think they're not queer, they think they're real macho. What a joke. The machos kill the others, and we have to stay here talking to police all night long, watching the clientele get scared away . . . and on top of that, putting up with coddled rich boys screaming 'murderer.'"

I took advantage of the end of his diatribe to ask: "Is the Indian a cross-dresser?"

"The Chilean? No way. He may be queer, but wearing women's clothes with that caveman look of his—out of the question. Not even my half-blind grandmother would believe he could be a woman."

"Are you sure? I suspect he's also had a go at being a transvestite."

"Not even if he wanted to. One of the reasons the Chilean was in demand around here is 'cause he was the poster boy for the muscular supermacho with a huge cock. The type of guy who's proud of his own dick. He hates women. Why would he try to pass for one?"

The question blew my theory out of the water. *Welcome back to square one*, I congratulated myself.

"What about the doctor?" I asked. "Did you know the doctor?"

"I never dated him, but he seemed to be a regular in the area. They say he was very professional, he liked taking it in the ass, and he paid top dollar. He was a good customer . . . Then he met the Indian and only wanted to date *him*. Poor guy got fucked."

"And why'd the Indian kill the doctor? Was he broke, something like that?"

"Beats me! The Chilean is crazy. They say he didn't even steal anything after killing the dude."

A car stopped beside us, but it wasn't a customer. It was the police. Typical cops, without the affability of Boris and Iório. They were young, which reinforced my theory that cops are like wine: the older, the better.

I was advised to go home, without opening my mouth on the way.

"We're investigating a homicide!" one of them bellowed through the car window.

"So am I," I responded, and headed home with that strange sensation of being observed.

I had a shot of Jack Daniel's and fell asleep to the deep voice of John Lee Hooker.

MAY 30

Wednesday

1

The homicide division was busy, with investigators frenetically coming and going. Reporters, with their irritating cameras, hovered around Boris's office like a swarm of bees. I was admitted to the room, escorted by an unpleasant young detective, after waiting in the hallway for five minutes. While waiting, I heard talk about the fugitive gringo, referred to as "the murderer"; Rafidjian was the "fag doctor." Inside the room, the atmosphere was a bit better, though Boris seemed on the brink of a breakdown, with his greasy hair uncombed, dark rings under his eyes visible through the thick lenses of his glasses, and the pallid skin of a smoker who hadn't slept for several days.

At that moment he was talking with Iório, who looked to be in a bad mood, perhaps from having gotten up early, and Stone, forever blasé and untrustworthy. The desk was covered with stacks of papers that grew by the minute as investigators kept arriving with new information.

A small writing pad with sayings of Seichō-No-Ie carried the phrase, *The man who climbs the mountain finds the sky.*

In spite of the swirling chaos, Boris appeared oblivious to everything except finding the where-abouts of the killer. He motioned me to a chair beside Iório, who barely managed to smile, and said, "If Miguel is in São Paulo, he'll be caught within twenty-four hours."

"And if he isn't?" I asked.

"I'll get him in a week. I've alerted the borders and the police throughout Brazil; he won't get away." He handed me a sheet with an artist's rendering of Miguel. The guy was an Indian, as we had established, and even in the impersonal and technical drawing (or perhaps because of it) looked menacing. The portrait, done with Stone's help, was in every precinct and all the newspapers. I concluded that the portrait eliminated any possibility of Miguel being a cross-dresser.

"Anything new, Bellini?" Boris asked.

"Nothing," I said.

He handed me a typed sheet and exchanged a complicitous glance with Iório. "Take a look at this."

"A dossier?"

He smiled. However friendly they might be, Boris and Iório were policemen before anything else. And police, by nature and tradition, always pride themselves on outdoing private detectives. I examined the paper.

Miguel Angel Sanchez Olivares, Chilean, has been living in the country illegally for more than four years. Approximate age: 26. Dark complexion, brown eyes, medium height, straight hair. Muscular physique. No marks or scars. No police record. Bisexual prostitute. Pimp, dancer in erotic shows and videos. Known in nightclubs in city center, in production offices of porn films, and the area of male prostitution near the Dante Alighieri School. No permanent address. He recently lived in the company of other male prostitutes in a building at 147 Alameda Glete, downtown area. He lived in Campo Grande, in the state of Mato Grosso, where he was known as Anjo and was also called the Indian. He has disappeared following the murder of Samuel Rafidjian Jr.

"How's that for a day's work?" boasted Boris.

I refrained from answering. Boris and Iório laughed. Stone appeared distant, as if anxious to get out of there.

"What about the guys he was living with on Alameda Glete?" I asked.

"They were checked out a little while ago. We made a surprise visit at six a.m. The guys, two prostitutes, didn't know anything." Boris lit a cigarette. "Miguel stayed there just four days, then he vanished with his things, which fit into a suitcase and a leather satchel. He left without letting anyone know, the day after the murder. He didn't even leave the money he'd promised to pay; the guys are pissed."

2

I called Dora from Boris's office and invited her for lunch at Almanara, an Arab restaurant. I had found myself suddenly interested in Lebanese culture. I checked my watch: 12:17. Since I had time (we had agreed on one o'clock), I walked over there. On the way, heading along Avenida São Luís, I thought about Beatrice, Beatriz's Lebanese grandmother. In a certain way there was a strong relationship between her and the Camelo pizzeria.

The Camelo was basically an Arab restaurant, but it still made the best pizza in the city. On weekends long lines formed in front of its doors on Rua Pamplona. It was ironic that in São Paulo, a city full of Italian immigrants, the best pizza was made by Arabs.

The city's cultural and racial composition never ceased to amaze me.

I reflected upon the professional alliance of Tufik and Khalid Tureg with Abel and Caruso Focca, Arabs and Italians working together to consolidate the Mafia in South America. Very poetic.

And why not me, Remo Bellini, and Beatriz Mekla united in the light of two cultures so different yet equally passionate and vibrant?

Beatriz.

The vision of her vagina as red as tuna sashimi (and I was correct, they did resemble one another), covered with dark hairs, wouldn't leave my head.

And I was thinking of Beatriz when I caught sight of the solid silhouette of Dora, sitting at the counter in the Almanara and drinking beer.

3

The waiter led us to a table; we sat down and ordered tabbouleh, raw kibbe, grape leaves, hummus, and Syrian bread. To drink: beer.

Dora, curious about Boris's discoveries, was put off when told of his progress. Ever since the Rafidjian case had begun to attract excessive publicity, along with personal intervention by the secretary of justice, the moods of Boris and Dora had become changeable and inversely proportional. Gradually, an unspoken competition was growing between them that only served to further incentivize them. The age-old rivalry of police versus detective. I asked: "You think the case will be solved?"

"Theoretically, yes. But some aspects remain unclear."

"For example?"

"Let's assume for the sake of argument that Rafidjian truly loved Miguel. Why would Miguel want to kill him?"

Before I could reply, Dora cut me off: "I know many crimes occur with no apparent motive. But statistics prove that crimes such as this normally happen immediately after a sexual relationship, and often involve the influence of alcohol and drugs."

"Suppose Miguel was blackmailing the doctor," I said. "Rafidjian seemed quite concerned with hiding his homosexuality."

"But why would a blackmailer lose his head enough to kill the victim with an umbrella?" Dora asked. "Wouldn't it be more reasonable, in this case, for Rafidjian to try to kill Miguel? And bumping someone off with an umbrella is by definition an emotional way of committing murder. All descriptions of Miguel suggest that he's closed off, cold, the type who would probably act with premeditation, carefully—the opposite of someone who would kill from passion."

"But you have to admit all the evidence is stacked against him," I said.

"Granted, but I'm going to direct my investigation toward a different angle. Listen"—she brought her head closer and lowered her voice—"I want you to find the two guys who were sharing an apartment with Miguel, and I also want you to locate Fatima and find out more from her about the friend who saw Rafidjian but refused to talk to the police. Let's leave the obvious work to Boris; what we're interested in now is finding out the apparently irrelevant details."

At times I had the impression that Dora read too much crime literature and had become a kind of Madame Bovary of noir fiction. After coffee, she went back to her mysterious tasks in the office (presumably including listening to interminable violin solos).

I took the bus to building 147 on Alameda Glete. The street, as we have seen, had a history: my first insipid sexual experience.

4

Building 147 was no different from the others in its deteriorated condition.

I opened a decaying wooden door and walked down a dark, poorly ventilated corridor to another decaying wooden door marked *Janitor*. I knocked. A middle-aged biracial man greeted me with a grunt: "Police?"

"More or less," I replied, without knowing what that meant. "I need to talk with the guys who lived here with the gringo who disappeared."

His body was half outside, holding the door ajar. "Apartment 206, but I don't think anybody's there now."

He was right. I knocked on the door of 206 and got no response. I returned to the janitor, stuck some money in his shirt pocket, handed him a slip of paper with the phone numbers of the office and my apartment, and said: "Ask them to get in touch with Detective Lobo or Detective Bellini urgently; it's in their interest to do so." I hoped the money would sing its siren song.

From there I went to the Hotel Mênfis, and since Fatima wasn't in either, I left a message for her to call me as soon as possible. I might have to offer sexual favors later, and that bothered me. I don't have to mention that certain phrases of Tulio Bellini and my ex-wife rang in my head, and when I went home in the middle of the afternoon, neither Albert King nor Jack Daniel's could rid me of the sensation that someone was following me. Maybe it was necessary, contrary to what I hoped, to telephone Zé Maria before the case was solved.

I went to sleep with the expectation that some phone call would wake me up.

5

But it was the doorbell, not the telephone, that woke me.

Fatima had a "very important" piece of news that she needed to convey "live." But first, as might be expected, she opened her blouse, aware of the effect (devastating) her large, firm breasts had on me. This time, unlike the previous, I confess I wasn't as impatient, but Fatima's wary attitude, which demanded payment in advance (if we consider that I paid with sex for the information she provided me), left me no alternative: we fucked again, and it was good.

She kept insisting on calling me Bel.

I was Remo to Beatriz and Bel to Fatima. *Remo Bel*, I thought, sounded affected, like a line of designer clothes for upper-class ladies. Remo Bel Couture.

My personality was disintegrating at a frightening pace.

The news that Fatima brought, however, really was important. She had located a friend of Miguel Angel who was willing to talk with me as long as the police weren't involved. His name was Juan. He had my phone number and would call me that same night. Fatima suspected Juan would ask for money in exchange for the information.

"These days nobody does anything for free," she said, smiling, and I felt like as much of a prostitute as Miguel Angel Sanchez Olivares.

6

Fatima lay in the bed, nude, for a long time, blowing smoke from a cigarette toward the ceiling. I was sitting in a chair beside the bed, also nude, trying to think of how to send her on her way. The lights were off, but the glare from the street coming in through the window was enough to illuminate the room.

Fatima stood up brusquely and said, "Don't worry, Bel, I'm leaving."

"Why?"

"You don't have to make up a story that your mother Livia is coming to visit you in the morning. I'm leaving now."

"What's this all about?" I asked.

"Nothing. You understand." She was on her feet, pulling on her panties. Her breasts were free, and I couldn't take my eyes off them. She said: "I just wanted to fuck. I like your cock."

I was flattered by the statement, not understanding why Lazarus arisen, which is what I called my dick, was having such success.

But my pride was to be short-lived.

After Fatima left, leaving behind the smell of cigarettes and sex, I was overcome by a powerful melancholy mixed with a discomfiting sense of rejection.

These were familiar sensations. They went back to a night almost two years before when I returned home to find a farewell note from my ex-wife, tossed onto our unmade bed. Since then I hadn't heard a word from her, except in visual and auditory hallucinations that, as if to make up for her absence, assailed me daily.

I was thinking about calling Zé Maria the next morning, when the telephone rang. A voice with a foreign accent said, "Bellini?"

"Speaking."

"It's Juan. Did Fatima mention me?"

"Yes."

"So," he said, "what's the deal?"

"What's the deal is *my* line. What do you want?" I asked.

"I wanna meet with you, but no police, you hear? No police involved."

"Understood. What else?"

"Nothing else," he said.

"You don't want money?"

"Just a little, to tide me over. I'm flat broke. But I'm not going to charge for the information." I could hear his smile, probably a cynical one. "Just slip me a little dough, that's all."

"Okay. And where do I find you?"

"Beside the statue of Luís de Camões in Trianon Park."

"Inside the park? At what time?"

"Midnight."

"Midnight? Impossible. The park is closed at night."

"I know," said Juan. "That way nobody will bother us while we talk."

"But I'll have to climb the fence," I protested.

"Just be discreet about it. If you bring anybody with you, you won't find me. Remember, tomorrow at midnight in Trianon Park beside the statue of Luís de Camões, the one-eyed guy."

He hung up.

MAY 31

Thursday

1

"**N**ew Facts About the Umbrella Crime: Murdered Doctor Was Homosexual." This sentence, with one variation or another, was printed in large letters on the front page of the city's major newspapers. Immediately below, in smaller type: "Discovery by Police Changes Course of Investigation."

The news invaded the crime section. The fact of Rafidjian being gay inexplicably elevated the case to a higher level of importance. Miguel's artist's sketch, depicting an Indian with fearsome features, also occupied a prominent position in the papers.

Cases like this, of gay men killed by rent boys, were relatively common in the crime pages; for this reason, when I arrived at the office for an emergency meeting called by Dora, the general atmosphere was one of "case closed."

Rita was excited, chatting with the intern responsible for the Pompilio Nagra–Fabian Fegri case. Though at the moment I was intensely involved with the "hunt for the Chilean killer" and had no time to even think about anything else, I asked the guy how my yuppie buddy Nagra was doing.

"You're not going to believe it, Bellini," Rita interjected.

"I'm not going to believe what?" I said.

She smiled at the intern: "Tell him!"

He looked at me, ill at ease, cleared his throat, and said, "The case is closed. Fabian settled accounts, saying he no longer needs Dora Lobo's services."

"Which means," I concluded, "that the entire story of betrayal was actually nothing but Fabian's paranoia?"

"You might say so," replied the intern.

Rita said: "Paranoia isn't the right word. Tell him."

The guy tried an awkward smile, stood up straight, and said, "They were in a relationship. They're living together now."

"Really?"

"Yeah. Fabian was in love with Pompilio, but I don't think he had the courage to say so. Deep down, what he wanted was to keep an eye on Pompilio, which he did with the pretense of suspecting he was cheating him professionally."

"And how did you discover this?"

"Two days ago they went out to dinner and had too much to drink; they left the restaurant arm in arm, caressing each other. Then they went to Fabian's house and didn't come out till the next day. Then they didn't go to work and instead spent all morning at home, and in the afternoon went to Ibirapuera Park for a picnic, where they behaved like two doves in love. Today I learned that they've moved in together, so the case is closed."

2

In her office, Dora was nervous, smoking and pacing the room. I asked, "Case closed?"

"Case closed? Have you gone crazy?"

"Does Sofia still want us on the case? Even after Stone's revelations?"

"Of course," Dora answered. "She didn't believe her husband cheated on her with women, much less with men. Besides which, until this Miguel is caught, there's nothing that proves he's really the killer."

"How can you say that, Dora? *More* proof? All that's missing is him confessing to the crime."

"They recognized Miguel's portrait in the building where Rafidjian had his office. A doorman remembered having seen a 'strange guy with the face of an Indian.' Miguel was there on the day and the hour of the crime."

"Then the case should be closed."

"No, that doesn't prove anything. Besides, Sofia Rafidjian called this morning and told me that until Miguel Angel himself confesses, we continue on the case. There's more," she said, raising her hand with the Tiparillo between her fingers. "We're staying on the case until I say who the guilty party is. That's what Sofia told me. She has complete confidence in me and will only accept the police's version if it matches my own."

Dora was eloquent, feverish, almost crazy. If I didn't know her so well, I'd even think she'd snorted a few lines of cocaine.

"But you don't doubt that Miguel is the killer, do you?" I asked.

"Yes, I do. Yesterday we still believed Miguel Angel and Ana Cíntia were the same person. Today we know they're not. The situation is still quite fluid . . . Who is Ana Cíntia Lopes, for example? There are also several other questions we don't have the answers to. Therefore, the case still isn't closed—and yes, I'm full of doubts."

"Very well. What's the next step?"

"What we need now is to get to Miguel before the police do."

"I have a surprise."

"What surprise?" she asked.

"A surprise is a surprise. I'll tell you tomorrow."

"If it has anything to do with the two guys who lived with him on Alameda Glete, you can forget it," she said. "They don't know anything, and the little they do know has already been checked out by the police."

"And what was it they knew?"

"Nothing. They needed someone to share the cost of rent and placed a sign on the ground floor of the building. Miguel appeared, left his things there, and promised he'd pay as soon as rent was due. The guys barely had a chance to meet him, he was almost never there except when he was sleeping like a hibernating bear, and he never spoke with anyone. Four days later he collected his gear and vanished." She smiled. "Boris wasted a lot of precious time chasing that dead end."

"Why do you and Boris play this childish cat-and-mouse game?"

"Because it makes things more interesting," she replied. Then she took an anxious drag on her Tiparillo. "What's the surprise, Bellini?"

"Tomorrow, I told you."

"Tell me, come on."

"No."

"Why?"

"Because it makes things more interesting."

3

At home, while waiting for midnight, I listened to Robert Johnson.

Since that ill-fated "night of omens" in Santos, I hadn't thought anymore about such things. In my mind, omens were linked to cocaine and therefore, despite Sherlock Holmes and Sigmund Freud, were best forgotten. But something in that unexpected coupling of Pompilio Nagra and Fabian Fegri put my senses on alert, like a dog that hears a distant sound and raises its ears.

Remo Bellini, the docile puppy. That was how Tulio Bellini and Dora Lobo saw me, like a tame and loyal dog. However much I barked and bared my teeth, to them I would always be a harmless pup. That was why, when I fired those fatal shots at Rocco, the guard dog at the Cubatão casino, I was also in a way killing the faithful little dog living inside me.

All that remained was for Tulio and Dora to realize it.

I wasn't pleased at Dora becoming so self-sufficient like she was that afternoon at the office. Which is why I never revealed anything about my secret meeting with Juan, Miguel Angel's friend, scheduled for

midnight that night in Trianon Park, near my building. Coincidence? Synchronicity? Omen? It didn't matter. The important thing was that Juan would meet
me based on my own investigative merits, even if those
merits occasionally included sexual favors with Fatima
screw it. Now that it was turning into a personal
competition between Dora and Boris, let them wait
for the revelations I would have tomorrow morning.

What's undeniable is that I couldn't come close
to guessing what was awaiting me at midnight amid
the dense foliage of Trianon Park.

4

It happened like this: at the appointed hour I walked
to the park, which was already closed, and climbed
the eight-foot fence. I was careful to choose a poorly
lit spot so as not to be seen by the hordes of cops in
the area. The strategy was sound, but I was so out of
shape that a simple climb became an awkward and
exhausting exercise.

Inside, I headed toward the Camões statue.
There was no one there, except for Camões himself,
who, mythic, phantasmagoric, and unreal, stared at
me with his one eye and smiled subtly as if foresee-
ing what was about to happen.

Then, before I realized it, I felt the cold pressure
of a knife blade on my neck.

"Juan?"

"Put the gun on the ground," he ordered in accented Portuguese.

I obeyed, and the guy relaxed his guard, allowing me to turn my face in his direction. But it wasn't Juan pointing the knife at me. I remembered Khalid and wondered whether, despite what he thought, men were an illusion too.

Facing me was Miguel Angel Sanchez Olivares, the Indian.

"You?" I blurted incredulously.

"Got a cigarette?" he asked.

"I don't smoke."

With his foot, he brought my Beretta closer until he could pick it up without moving the knife or taking his eyes off me. He quickly examined it, unloaded it efficiently, and said: "Nice automatic." Then, as a peace gesture, he returned the unloaded gun, holding it by the barrel and offering me the butt. "I don't want to hurt you," he said, "I was just afraid you wouldn't let me explain . . ."

"Explain what?" I asked.

"Explain that I didn't kill Rafidjian."

Miguel Angel, the most wanted man in the city, whose artist's rendition appeared in newspapers, police precincts, and bus stations, stood in front of me, looking weary and defenseless. He was wearing denim pants and shirt, and white sneakers. His clothes were dirty. He hadn't shaved in several days, his dark hair was disheveled, and his eyes were red.

"I didn't kill Rafidjian," he repeated. Putting the knife away, he sat down on the ground and dropped his head into his hands. "I didn't kill the guy! I didn't kill him." Miguel raised his head and looked at me. "And you're the only one who can help me."

"Me? Take it easy, buddy. To begin with, how do you know who I am?"

"From the newspapers."

"And who's Juan?" I asked.

"Juan's a friend who's helping me. He's the one who talked me into finding you."

"And so he's the guy who called me?"

"Yes."

"And who was tailing me, you or Juan?"

"Me. My idea was to talk to you, but I was afraid you'd get scared and ruin everything."

"Then your friend Juan got the brilliant idea to lure me into this trap?"

"Yeah, but don't take it the wrong way, dude, this is my last chance."

"Chance at what?"

"Bellini, I ain't got much time, the cops are gonna catch me at any moment. And once they do, they're never gonna let me out of there . . . You gotta listen to me."

"I'm listening."

"That day, when I got to Rafidjian's office, he was already dead."

"And why didn't you tell that to the police?"

"Because they would never have believed me."

"And why do you think I will?"

"I don't think you will, but I gotta try."

"Then try," I said, under the watchful good eye of Camões.

JUNE 1

Friday

1

I arrived at the office elegantly dressed, wearing cologne, clean shaven, and a complete master of the situation. At that moment I had pulled into the lead on the Rafidjian case and, surprisingly, had left my competitors Dora and Boris in the dust in the home stretch.

When I called Dora, some hours earlier, to inform her that the surprise I had alluded to the day before was progressing well—and that the surprise represented a resolution of the case—she nearly had a heart attack and ordered me back to the office immediately.

Dora expressed indignation at not having been included in my secret meeting with Juan, but then she made no effort to hide her joy at finding out that it was not Juan but Miguel Angel who had appeared at the park. This time it was she who remained silent, nervously smoking her Tiparillos, while I narrated what had occurred the night before in Trianon

Park. After relating the unexpected encounter with the murder suspect, and his denial of having committed the crime, I explained how Miguel Angel justified his story.

"'Everything they say about me is true, Bellini,' Miguel told me, and I felt like a priest hearing confession. 'Ever since I arrived from Chile four years ago, I've made my living by turning tricks, and I don't deny that to anyone.'

"I said, 'Nor could you, since it's already more than evident.'

"'That's the problem. All the evidence is against me.'

"'And you still want me to help you get out of this? Why me?' I asked, but he continued talking as if I hadn't said a word.

"'All these years I've lived by screwing fags and older women. I did a few shows too, I met people and made some contacts. I led my life, trying to get my act together, but I didn't get anywhere.'"

Dora cut in: "Leave the reflections aside and just stick to the facts, Bellini."

"Hey, I'm just trying to emulate your style," I countered.

"If that's my style," she said, blowing smoke out her nose, "I can imagine what goes on when you have to listen to me. Continue, please."

I tried to make the account more objective, eliminating my own observations. "Miguel said: 'That was when I met Rafidjian, and he fell in love with me. I liked it at first, because he gave me dough, presents, and I thought I'd struck it rich, guaranteed my future, understand?' I said I did, and he went on: 'But the business started getting weird. Rafidjian wanted exclusivity, he wanted me only for him. Even though the money was welcome, I couldn't accept the role of a rich man's lover—that wasn't why I had come to Brazil. Besides, I'm not even that into guys—I just fuck them to make money. And I only pitch, I don't catch. But Rafidjian sometimes treated me like a woman and that pissed me off. The time came when I had to say enough. My life was half crazy. A girl had gotten pregnant with a child of mine, Dinéia—'

"'What?' I interrupted. 'Dinéia was pregnant with your child?'

"'That's right. And I just found out she lost the child. My life is complete shit.'"

"Interesting," commented Dora.

"He said that Dinéia getting pregnant affected him so much that he resolved to change his life. He decided to put an end to his affair with Rafidjian. Except that, knowing Rafidjian wouldn't accept the breakup easily, he had to come up with some sort of plan."

"One moment, Bellini." Dora stood up, went to the liquor cabinet, and served herself a glass of port. Then she returned to her desk. "Go on, please."

"Miguel said, 'I needed to invent something to appeal to the old man, then I realized he only thought about love, only talked about love—he was a romantic. Here's what I did: the last time we dated, I told him, *Rafidjian, I'm getting married. I'm in love with a girl and I'm gonna get married.*'

"'How can that be? Who is she?' Rafidjian asked him.

"'Ana Cíntia Lopes, a dancer at the Dervish.'"

"And who is Ana Cíntia Lopes?" asked Dora, exasperated, interrupting the flow of my memory.

"Keep calm."

2

"*Ana Cíntia Lopes* was the first name that came into Miguel Angel Sanchez Olivares's head when he made up the story that he was about to marry a dancer at the Dervish. But the name itself wasn't invented. Ana Cíntia actually existed. Miguel met her in Chile when he was a child. Ana Cíntia Lopes was a Brazilian girl who lived on the same street as Miguel Angel, in a poor district in Santiago. He was in love with her at the time, and Ana Cíntia remained etched in his memory as his first love. Her name therefore immediately came to mind when he needed to supply the identity of an imaginary woman he would supposedly marry."

"'And what's she like?' asked Rafidjian when he received the news.

"And so Miguel, who had a photo of Camila in his wallet ('because she worked with me, because we dated, and most of all because she was so luscious'), showed it to Rafidjian and said, 'This is her. This is Ana Cíntia Lopes. She works at the Dervish, but she's fed up with that life, just like me, so we decided to ditch everything and get married.'

"It wasn't by chance that Miguel showed Rafidjian a photo of Camila. He knew she had left the Dervish and returned to her father's home in Santos. So if Rafidjian checked the story, he wouldn't be able to find Camila and try to dissuade her from marrying Miguel, which would ruin the plan. The fact of Dinéia resembling Camila and her having left at the same time for Cornélio Procópio with his child in her belly was, according to Miguel, 'a total coincidence, since Dinéia wasn't even part of the plan.'"

"Very well," said Dora. "That was Miguel's strategy: giving a false name to a dancer who he knew couldn't be found in the city, for the purpose of making Rafidjian believe he was getting married and changing his life. So what happened next?"

"Miguel actually did try to change his life. He went to live in an apartment with Chilean friends, and for a good period of time stopped frequenting the places he was accustomed to, places where Rafidjian would surely go to look for him. But according to Miguel: 'After a month, I was dead broke and missed the nightlife. The first thing I did was leave my friends' apartment and find a hole on Alameda Glete. Then I decided to bring Rafidjian back into play and get some dough outta him. I knew the old guy was totally paranoid about the possibility of people finding out he was gay, so I called him at home and applied pressure. He used to go crazy when anyone called him at home. It was forbidden. That kind of hookup had to be through the office—Mondays, Tuesdays, and Wednesdays, between noon and one o'clock, lunchtime—when he was by himself. I called Sunday night to rattle the old guy, and did a sort of blackmail, saying I would out him to his friends unless he gave me some coin.'

"'*A sort of blackmail?* Explicit blackmail, you mean,' I said, and Miguel Angel got a bit uptight.

"'Yeah,' he told me, 'Rafidjian was pissed, but at the same time he was happy, because he really missed me. He asked me to go to his office the next day, at the usual time, and I thought he was gonna cough up some green. But when I showed up, the old man was dead on the floor, all bloody, with his eyes gouged out. I got the hell outta there fast.'

"'And what did you do then?' I asked.

"'I ran away,' Miguel said, 'I tried to get some money together to leave the city but couldn't scrounge up enough. I was desperate, so I hid out at some friends' house, waiting for the police to tie me to the crime. I know they're not gonna believe my story.'

"'It's difficult for them to believe,' I agreed, 'but who else could have killed the doctor?'

"'I don't have the slightest idea, and that's why I came up with this meeting. I know you work with Detective Lobo, and you're the only one who can get me out of this mess. The problem is, I don't have any money to pay for your services, but when I do, I swear I'll pay everything. Speaking of which, can you give me that payment?'

"'What payment?'

"'What Juan asked you for on the phone.'

"'Do I look like a fool?' I asked.

"'No more than I do,' he said. 'Somebody set a trap for me and I fell in it like a sucker.'

"I gave him some change and he left, edging his way along the park's shrubbery like his life was on the line."

3

For a moment, the smoke from the Tiparillo looked almost cinematic, transporting the action from Trianon Park to the Itália Building.

In Dora's office: "So now you're the accomplice of a fugitive."

"Don't give me a hard time. You ought to be congratulating me."

"And I do. Thanks to you, we can deduce that Rafidjian's intention was to find Miguel Angel, but because he was fearful we would discover his homosexuality he hired us to find Ana Cíntia, so that he could locate Miguel without letting on he was gay."

"The problem was that Rafidjian actually believed Miguel had married Ana Cíntia," I added, "when it was just something the Chilean made up."

"That's why we followed so many false leads," Dora said. "Miguel Angel merged fantasy and reality to create his story and deceive Rafidjian, and that made our work more difficult. The curious thing is that the entire story was fictitious. To find Miguel, the dancer Rafidjian sought out was Camila, but he thought her name was Ana Cíntia, which in turn was the name of a childhood friend of Miguel's. And Dinéia, despite having Miguel Angel's child in her belly, had nothing to do with the story. Even Camila herself, though used by the Chilean in his scheme, never knew she was in the middle of all this confusion. Ingenious!"

"Quite so," I said. "The guy made so much up that in the end he found himself trapped in a web of his own making. If, that is, we accept the premise that he's innocent in the doctor's death."

"I believe he is. The man wouldn't risk meeting with you at the park without good reason."

"But if we believe that," I said, "we're back at square one." "Did we ever leave it?" Dora asked.

4

I asked: "Dora, who was Samuel Rafidjian Jr. really?"

"It's hard to define a man in a few words. But Rafidjian was an insecure guy, a dreamer. It's no accident that I nicknamed him Don Quixote the day I met him. He had to invent a parallel reality to escape the oppressive atmosphere of his own home. I don't blame him for that. Life beside those two strong-willed and antagonistic women must have been unbearable. Not to mention those strange, spoiled children."

"Can you explain further?"

"In the first place there's Sofia, the widow. She's delicate, well-mannered, and borders on unpleasant. She's a woman with a degree in psychology who opted not to work, in order to live for her children and her husband. She's vain but aware of her function of homemaking and child rearing. She has a rigid moral code and, from what I've observed, was totally ignorant of her deceased husband's extramarital affairs. I can only imagine the difficulty she must have processing the news that her husband was gay. Her bourgeois and conservative upbringing will never let her forgive him."

"One final detail," I said. "Sofia and Rafidjian's mother, Dona Soaila, never got along."

Dora lit a new Tiparillo, then continued: "The second woman is Ismalia, the maid. She's the tall lady who was consoling the two younger children at Rafidjian's funeral. Remember?"

I nodded.

"Ismalia has worked as the Rafidjian family maid since Samuel was still single. When he married Sofia, Ismalia accompanied the couple as part of the wedding present from Rafidjian's parents. There was always a veiled power struggle between Ismalia and Sofia. First, because Ismalia had a good relationship with Dona Soaila, Rafidjian's mother, and also because the younger children were very close to her—unlike Samuel III, the older son, who was very close to his mother. Their differences go beyond that. While Sofia is a delicate and discreet woman, Ismalia is a rancorous, disagreeable busybody. Still, I can't deny that Ismalia helped me more than anyone to better understand the Rafidjian family, since no one was as willing to talk as she was. Though she's quite a gossip, she seemed not to have suspected any extramarital activity on Rafidjian's part."

"What about the spoiled children?" I asked.

"Samuel III, who goes by *Samuca*, is quiet and introverted. But he always comes across as attentive with his mother and his siblings. He's studious and wants to pursue the same career as his father. He also likes to play basketball—in fact, studying and basketball are his only pastimes. Silvia, the young girl, is by far the oddest of all. Like her older brother, she's very fond of sports. She has played tennis since she was quite little and even won a few junior tournaments at the Pinheiros Club. She's quiet and insincere and has a bad temper, like her mother. At first she refused to talk to me, but when her mother ordered her to cooperate, Silvia obeyed, though in a defiant manner. She appears to have suffered greatly from the death of her father. Finally, there's Serginho, the kid brother. Serginho is the one who is most like his father. He's a simple little kid with no personality. But he's reticent and, strange as it sounds, quite hypocritical for a ten-year-old."

"A ten-year-old child can't be a hypocrite."

"He is a hypocrite. Don't underestimate children, Bellini. They're capable of unimaginable atrocities."

I couldn't believe that Dora held such an opinion of Serginho, a chubby, harmless boy I had met at Rafidjian's funeral. I asked: "What about Rafidjian's friends? Did any of them suspect his homosexuality?"

"Not at all. His friends are as fake and self-absorbed as he was. They all said Samuel was a 'great friend, a skilled professional, and a wonderful son, husband, and father'—a bunch of liars. It doesn't surprise me that a man like Rafidjian, trapped between two annoying women, three insincere children, and various idiotic friends, opted to look for fun elsewhere. Nothing could be more natural."

"He didn't have some close friend, someone more intimate?"

"The only one who demonstrated a somewhat deeper understanding of Rafidjian's personality was Ivan Boudeni, his former professor and, from what I could glean, a kind of confidant. Boudeni confirmed that Rafidjian was a truly talented surgeon and a man of great sensitivity, but at the same time his behavior was unstable and unpredictable. Rafidjian sought out Boudeni whenever he experienced bouts of depression, which were far from rare. But he never confessed his homosexuality. His conversations were basically about medicine and his family."

We said nothing for a moment. I broke the silence: "Do you have a suspect, Dora?"

"No. But I've noticed that lately certain people have been behaving suspiciously."

"How so?"

"Sofia, the widow, for instance. She's so plainly innocent that, in my view, it becomes suspicious. No one is that unsuspicious. Then there's Ismalia . . . Despite its being a cliché, we mustn't forget the example of detective novels, in which the butler—"

"What's with this, Dora?" I cut in. "You putting me on?"

"No, I'm serious."

"Don't you think you're being a bit fantastical?"

"But that's how I learned to solve crimes— through literature."

Maybe the conversation was becoming too philosophical. Or pathetic. Even so, I pressed, "What about the children?"

"The children . . . My dear, if they were mine I'd put them all in a psychiatric clinic. I don't trust the mental health of any of them. Frankly, it wouldn't shock me if that fat little monster killed his own father."

"You've got it in for the boy," I said.

That was when I realized Dora was having fun at my expense. And what's worse, I was playing the role of patsy. She liked to do that when she was tired or irritated. Before solving a case, Dora always showed signs of stress. It was as if her brain worked better under pressure—though she would never admit it.

"Enough fooling around, Dora. I'm being serious."

"If you're so serious, tell me who *your* suspect is."

"Dona Glaucia, the secretary," I said.

"For the love of God, Bellini. You say you're being sincere and then you come up with Dona Glaucia? Not even a dumb cop would believe she could have committed the crime. Speaking of police"—she took a deep drag from her Tiparillo—"don't you dare give Boris even a hint of your conversation with Miguel Angel. I want to keep that advantage."

"Let's make a deal," I proposed. "If I don't say anything to Boris, you tell me something more about the *suspicious* behavior of the Rafidjians. But speak honestly."

"That's known as blackmail," she said.

"Indeed."

5

Dora's uneasiness gave away a brutal anxiety. But then she accepted the deal.

"Ever since Rafidjian was killed, members of the family have been adopting strange habits. Sofia, the widow, has started watching television all day. Before her husband died, she hated television and discouraged her children from watching it. And now she watches it day and night. Silvia, the girl, is more withdrawn than normal and spends her days shut inside her bedroom. She doesn't leave even to play tennis, which is impressive when you consider her love of the sport. Samuca, the oldest, is paranoid and suspicious of everybody in the house. Since the day his father died, he hasn't let Ismalia clean his room or prepare his food or even wash his clothes, preferring to do it all himself. And Ismalia now talks to herself at night. She says she's speaking to the spirits and that she has communicated regularly with Rafidjian. He hasn't revealed to her the name of his killer, but Ismalia promises it's only a matter of time."

"What about Serginho?"

"Serginho is acting normal."

"And just what does that mean?" I asked.

"I don't know. If you find out, please tell me."

JUNE 2

Saturday

I decided to make some free time and promised myself not to speak (even mentally) the names Rafidjian, Miguel Angel, Boris, and Dora.

I also promised myself something else, and I achieved it that night, in a bar.

"Beatriz, can we get serious about seeing each other?"

"What do you mean, Remo?"

We were sitting facing each other, drinking margaritas.

"You know, get more involved."

"Sometimes I don't think you take me seriously, man. I'm not going to get involved with you. I couldn't get involved with you—even if I wanted to."

"Why? Because of some man in the past? Haven't you been in therapy since you were a child to overcome that trauma?"

"You don't understand. It's not a thing of the past—it's of the present too."

"You're married!" I exclaimed. "I should have known."

"Don't be silly, Remo. Why do you have to act like an old-fashioned, possessive guy who wants to get serious and then get married? You're obsessed with the idea of marriage! And besides, things are so cool the way they are . . . It's all happened without us forcing anything. Why formalize something so spontaneous?"

This was a typical speech from a university student, and I had to appeal to my own maturity. "You don't want to get tied down to a traditional relationship because you think you're too young and have a lot of living to do before making a commitment to an older man—is that it?"

"What older man, huh? You're more of a child than I am."

"Just imagine: I'm disillusioned, abandoned, scarred by life. From where I am, it seems clear that youth is an illusion."

"*From where I am?* Are you crazy? You're thirty-two and think you know everything . . . You're like my father."

"You're right," I said. "Maturity is also an illusion. Actually, everything lately seems like an illusion to me."

"This isn't an illusion," she whispered, and

leaned forward and stuck her tongue in my ear.

"No, it isn't."

She put her hand on my dick under the table and said, "Let's leave things the way they are, with no obligations."

Once again my best intentions to commitment and to unveiling a feminine mystery went up in smoke.

That night Beatriz and I had sex, which I, revealing a conservative and outmoded facet of my personality, inexplicably insisted on calling *love*. I eagerly penetrated her tuna sashimi, and for the first time, in a disturbingly experienced way, she sucked my dick. It made me a slave for life.

Men are always disarmed when women they're in love with demonstrate ability in the sacred art of fellatio.

Early the next morning, despite my insistence that she stay, Beatriz left. She explained that she always spent Sundays with her father since he couldn't stand them. "Me neither," I offered, but it wasn't enough to make her stay. Women are strange. After we screwed, Fatima always wanted to stay and I would ask her to leave. Beatriz, on the other hand, wanted to leave and I would ask her to stay. I thought about my ex-wife, which was natural: whenever I felt re-jected, she returned from the depths of my memory, not to console but to leave me even more depressed.

I recalled Khalid's theory again: women had nothing in common except the fact that they were an illusion. They also always did exactly the opposite of what I expected them to do.

JUNE 3

Sunday

I spent the day uselessly, lying in bed reading newspapers and listening to the blues.

Listening to the blues on a sunny Sunday afternoon in São Paulo (in this case accompanied by the neighbors' radio broadcasting soccer matches and game shows) is one step from suicide. Especially when you have, as I did, a pistol within reach.

For me, a Sunday was like a long desert to be crossed.

One more Sunday conquered by Remo the Survivor—that's what I was thinking when Dora phoned around ten that night.

"Bellini, Boris just called. Miguel Angel has been arrested."

"What happened?"

"The police raided a small apartment in Bixiga where close to thirty Chileans lived piled on top of one another, most of them in the country illegally.

Miguel was there. He didn't resist arrest and refused to make a statement."

"Is he at homicide?"

"Yes."

"Should I go there?"

"No," Dora replied. "He's incommunicado. We can't see him till tomorrow."

"Why is that?"

"To jerk our chain."

JUNE 4

1

When I got to the precinct, I was greeted by a dark-skinned guy who extended his hand toward me. "My name is Juan."

"Nice to meet you."

"Forgive me for making up that story about a meeting, but now more than ever you're the only chance for Miguel to get out of this mess."

I would have liked to continue the conversation and tell the guy I wasn't anybody's last chance, much less Miguel's, but then a couple waved to me, catching my attention.

It was Duilio, the sailor/taxi driver from Santos. Hugging him like an affectionate girlfriend was Camila Garcia, the mysterious dancer and junkie. It was an intense and destabilizing surprise. Duilio came toward me.

"Boss, Camila is anxious to meet you."

And she, beautiful and enigmatic: "So it was you who was following me?"

"You're . . . ?"

"We're together," Duilio confirmed, embracing her. "And we like to say that you were our Cupid."

"Yeah, our Cupid, ha ha," Camila chimed in, smiling with glassy eyes.

At that instant, Dinéia emerged through the front door and Camila moved to greet her. I took advantage of her absence to ask Duilio: "Forgive the lack of discretion, but weren't you married to Sintra's daughter?"

"I still am, but Eugenia doesn't know anything, and Camila isn't the jealous type."

"I figured. And how's Sintra been doing?"

"The old man is fine. He follows the case in the newspapers."

"How did all this happen?" I asked.

"What? Our thing?"

"Yeah."

"It was 'cause of you. You were our Cupid, boss."

"Cupid . . . That's a good one, Duilio. I can't manage to find a girlfriend for myself, and you call me Cupid."

"Here's what happened," he said. "After you left Santos, I grew curious to know who you were following. I remembered the address, 63 Rua Tratado de Tordesilhas. So I snorted a few lines and started playing detective. Between us, Camila is divine. I fell in love, asked her out, that sort of thing . . . and I discovered she goes for the same kind of stuff I do, get it?"

"How so?"

"Eugenia, my wife, doesn't like me snorting coke or drinking—I gotta pretend I'm straight all the time when I'm not, and that's not cool. With Camila it's different. We snort, we drink, and afterward"—he smiled maliciously like a typical macho—"she fucks real good, boss, and I mean *real* good."

Despite finding the conversation a bit awkward, I confess I felt envious of Duilio. Not just because of the sex (which judging by Camila's appearance must really have been quite good) but also the mixture of sex and cocaine, which I remembered as being superb.

"Let's go meet Dinéia," he said, and I imagined that perhaps Duilio had intentions more interesting than my own.

2

It was the first time in my life that I'd seen Dinéia in the flesh, but I greeted her like an old friend.

She said: "You were watching us, it's like in a movie . . . so exciting!"

Camila, who was finding everything amusing, guffawed.

Only when a policeman generously reminded us to keep quiet did I remember we were walking down a hallway in homicide, which led me to ask Camila, Dinéia, and Duilio the following question: "What are you all doing here?"

Camila said: "We came for the . . ."

"The confrontation," Duilio supplied.

"Confrontation—ha ha ha," Camila said, clearly enjoying herself.

"Don't pay any attention to her," said Dinéia, addressing me. "She's crazy." Then she grasped Camila, who was still laughing, by the shoulders. "Behave yourself, Camilinha. If the guys called us here it must be for something serious." She turned back to me. "I received a summons yesterday in Cornélio."

"Cornélio, ha ha ha ha ha ha . . ." Camila was laughing uncontrollably, as if she were having an attack of hysteria.

Duilio led her to the water fountain. "This chick needs to cool her head," he said.

I was alone with Dinéia now and didn't waste the opportunity: "Is it true the baby you were expecting was Miguel Angel's?"

"What kind of question is that? What gives you the right to ask me such a thing?"

"It's important, Dinéia, very important."

"Why?"

"Because it may help Miguel."

"And who said I want to help that animal?" asked Dinéia.

"It's not a question of wanting to or not, it's a question of justice," I argued.

She looked at me in silence.

"Was the child Miguel's, Dinéia?" I repeated.

"Yes, it was. I mean, I think it was."

"But did you tell Miguel you thought the child was his?"

"No . . . I told him I was *certain*."

"Very good."

"How come?" she asked.

"You've just given me an important indication that Miguel isn't a liar, and that he's also probably innocent—"

"Huh?"

Before I could explain, a young and unpleasant detective (the one I had met earlier) approached and said, "Remo Bellini? The chief wants to speak with you."

In his office, Boris received me standing. He was jubilant. His hair was wet and combed back, like a ghost just out of the shower. Behind his thick glasses, his eyes were more sunken than ever. "So you haven't yet congratulated me on closing the case."

"What, did the Indian confess?"

"Not yet. But do you have any doubt he killed the doctor?" Boris asked.

"I do," I said. "Can I speak to him?"

"Help yourself, but make it quick. Very quick." He lit another cigarette. "I'll confront him and then present him to the press myself. The secretary of justice is coming to witness it in person."

While the unpleasant detective led me to Miguel's cell, I imagined Dora inventing another killer, just to avoid admitting a mistake.

Miguel Angel Sanchez Olivares was quiet, alone in a special cell.

I felt like I was looking at a man without hope.

3

"If you want help," I said, "you have to help me too."

"What help can I give you, man, locked up in here, when out there everybody says I'm an insane killer who murdered a man with an umbrella?"

"If you didn't kill Rafidjian, then who did?" I asked.

"I don't know. I've been busting my brain thinking about it."

"Some enemy trying to frame you?"

"I don't have enemies," he replied. "Or friends."

"What about Juan?"

"Juan is a brother. You know what it is to have a brother, man?'

"No."

"Or a friend?" he said. "Do you know what it means to have a friend?"

"No again. But I know what it is to have a father, if that's worth anything."

"That I can't say. I never had a father."

At that moment the unpleasant young detective shouted, "Time!"

"Already? One last question." I whispered to the Chilean. "What does Juan think of all this?"

Before Miguel could answer, the detective intervened, pointing to his wristwatch. "Time's up, my brother."

I hated having to put up with the guy calling me "brother." I turned to Miguel and said, "I'll be back."

On the way outside, I ran into Camila and Dinéia again.

"You two nearly drove me crazy," I said as I approached them.

They both smiled, apparently flattered.

Dinéia asked: "What's this about Miguel being innocent?"

"Miguel? Innocent? Ha ha ha," Camila remarked sarcastically.

I turned to Dinéia: "Innocent enough to believe the child in your belly was his."

"What child?" asked Camila.

"That's not innocence, it's presumption," said Dinéia, ignoring Camila.

"Cupid, who are you talking about?" Camila asked me.

"We're talking about life, my love," I replied.

"Oh good. I thought you were talking about *me*."

"Well, in a certain way, we were," I said.

"Talking about Camila?" Dinéia asked. "I wasn't talking about Camila!"

"It doesn't matter," I said.

"It does matter!" insisted Dinéia.

"Why?"

"Because you men think that all women are alike. That's why you treat us this way."

"Like an illusion?" I asked.

"No," she answered, "like a bunch of idiots."

I walked away.

Back at the office, Dora was closeted in her room with Ismalia, the Rafidjians' maid. Dora had given the express order for them not to be interrupted, so I left a written report on the latest developments and headed home. First, I stopped at the August Moon for a salami-and-provolone sandwich on French bread and cold beer (or four, as it turned out).

Antonio asked, "So then, Bellini, having a party tomorrow?"

"Party?"

I had forgotten, but the next day was my thirty-third birthday.

4

Fatima had acquired a new habit. Instead of phoning ahead, she now came directly to my place when she wanted to see me. And as soon as I opened the door, without saying a word, she would show me her breasts. Subjugated by some magnetic force, I prostrated myself before that pair of breasts like a famished baby. Naturally, this innocent pastime degenerated into a more adult form of amusement.

That was what happened that Monday night on the eve of my birthday: Fatima showed up and we screwed.

After midnight I said, "Today I'm thirty-three."

Fatima: "Then I'm going to give you a present."

We were in bed, naked. She made me lie on her lap, then offered me one of her breasts and said, "Suck."

I obeyed. As I sucked, she jacked me off intensely.

I came.

"Did you like the present?" she asked.

"Know something, Fatima? You're my friend."

"I really am, Bel. Didn't you realize that before?"

"No. But now that we're friends, can I ask something of you?"

She nodded.

"Don't call me Bel. It's ridiculous."

"Ridiculous, Bellini? You're being insecure."

"Insecure?"

"Yeah. What's the problem if I call you Bel? It's an affectionate nickname."

"It makes me feel like an idiot. Bel is ridiculous. If anyone hears it, it could damage my reputation."

"Reputation? What reputation?" she challenged.

"I'm a detective, girl."

"So what? Can't detectives have nicknames?"

"Sure. But not Bel."

"All right, all right. You're no fun." She lit a cigarette. "Speaking of detectives, did you know Miguel Angel was arrested?"

"I was with him today at the precinct," I said.

"What about Juan? Did he call you that night?"

"Yes. How do you know Juan?"

"He came to me. I don't know how, but Juan found out that I was looking for information about Miguel Angel. He tracked me down at the Dervish and asked why I was investigating Miguel, and I told him it was to help you. Then he asked me to put him in contact with you."

"Does Juan work the night shift?" I asked.

"No, I don't think so."

Afterward, Fatima and I remained in bed, silent. That night, oddly, I didn't feel like asking her to leave. She must have noticed, because she asked: "You have a girlfriend, don't you? Is that why you don't like me sleeping here? You're afraid your fiancée will find out?"

"Fiancée my ass. I don't even have a girlfriend."

"Then how come you usually kick me out right after fucking me?"

"Because I'm in love with a girl named Beatriz," I confessed.

"Poor Bellini. This Beatriz clearly isn't good for you, since she's making you a nervous wreck."

"No, she's cool. The problem is that Beatriz doesn't want to commit, while I want a more stable relationship, understand?"

"I understand."

Fatima stood up and started getting dressed.

"Don't you want to stick around?" I asked.

"Not today," she said, and promptly left.

JUNE 5

Tuesday

1

As she did every fifth of June, my mother called. "Congratulations, Remo. Thirty-three, Christ's age." Livia Bellini had the ability to link any topic to religion.

"Thank you, Mother. I hope not to be crucified this year."

"Of course not; but your mother knows the via dolorosa that has been your life."

"There is no via dolorosa; my life is great. I'm doing what I like."

"Your father suffers so much . . ."

"He suffers because he's selfish and can't accept the fact that his son lives his own life."

"Don't talk like that."

"All right, let's drop it."

"Have you been eating?" she asked.

"Yes."

"Reminho, why don't you take advantage of this

date and assume an attitude worthy of Jesus Christ?"

"What attitude?" I asked, anticipating the response.

"Reestablish a relationship with your father. Speak with him."

"But he's the one who doesn't want to speak to me."

"A father is something very important in life," she said.

"I know. Have you told *him* that yet?"

"Yes. And he asked me the same thing—if I had talked to you. You two are so alike, Remo."

"Don't say that, Mother. Did you call on my birthday to insult me?"

"Heaven forbid! You know how I suffer because of that."

"Sorry."

"God gave me two sons and took one of them away from me too soon. You're the only one I have left, and now at this age I have to suffer the pain of my son refusing to speak to his own father?"

"But he also refuses to speak to *me*."

"Because you're both proud. Two proud, hard-headed men! If either of you had the generosity to deign to speak to the other, this foolishness would come to an end—a father and son not on speaking terms, what a calamity!"

"Someday he'll understand me and accept me," I said. "Don't worry. What matters is that I'm happy."

"What about your health?"

"Excellent."

"Don't forget to eat well."

"Okay."

"So, happy birthday, Reminho."

"Thanks, Mother. May I ask you for something?"

"What?"

"Don't call me Reminho again. Please."

2

I had breakfast at the August Moon.

When I asked for the check, Antonio smiled and said, "No check. Consider it a birthday present."

Afterward, as if in commemoration of the occasion, I bought all the day's newspapers and went back home. I put on Muddy Waters, poured a Jack Daniel's with water and ice, and stretched out on the bed in the company of the day's news.

The main story was the arrest of Miguel Angel Sanchez Olivares, "the umbrella killer." There was speculation as to the motive of the crime—"probably a misunderstanding stemming from blackmail of which the doctor was supposedly the victim"—and the Chilean's confession was expected imminently. In a photo, Boris appeared circumspect beside the secretary of justice. "The crime is all but solved," declared the secretary in a caption beneath the photo.

To me the crime was still a long way from being solved, but I was wrong, as proved by a phone call I received immediately afterward.

"Happy birthday, Bellini."

"Dora?"

"I've got a present for you."

"What is it?"

"It's a surprise. But I'll give you a couple of hints. First, be here at six o'clock sharp. Second, have you ever heard of the two riddles of the Sphinx of Thebes?"

"No."

"Too bad. If you knew of the Sphinx of Thebes, maybe you'd discover, before six, who killed Rafidjian."

"What are you talking about?"

"I've figured out who the killer is, but I won't announce the name until six o'clock here in the office. You'll understand why later."

"You're kidding, Dora."

"I'm not kidding. Be here at—"

"Six o'clock. I got it. But what does the Sphinx of Thebes have to do with it?"

"Everything. Investigate, and maybe you'll show up here without curiosity."

"But—"

"Happy birthday, Bellini."

Before she hung up, I heard Paganini playing furiously in the background.

Dora and her riddles, I thought. *Son of a bitch*.

I checked my watch: 11:42.

I had a little over six hours to try to solve that idiotic riddle. Though women have always told me riddles, I've never been able to solve them. So I decided to go to a library, any library—the Municipal Library, perhaps, or maybe even the law school library—to look up *Sphinx* or *Thebes* or even *Riddle* in an encyclopedia.

Could it be that simple?

I took a cold shower and shaved. While I dressed, I pondered: *What if the riddles of the Sphinx of Thebes were something like the Pythagorean theorem? Or Archimedes's principle? Wasn't Archimedes the guy who yelled "Eureka!" in his bathtub?*

"Eureka!" I myself shouted, remembering where I knew (vaguely) the riddles of the Sphinx of Thebes from: the bookcase in Tulio Bellini's office! More precisely, from the *Dictionary of Classical Mythology*. I would have to immediately dash to the office of my father, with whom I hadn't spoken for over a year, to unlock the secrets that would lead me to the name of the killer of Samuel Rafidjian Jr. And all this was happening on June 5, the day I turned thirty-three.

* * *

Lacking the courage to face my father (even more so with the banal motive of consulting a dictionary of mythology), I phoned his office before running out like a maniac. Dona Helga, his longtime secretary, answered.

"Dr. Remo?"

"How are you, Helga? Is my father there?"

"No sir. He has a hearing in court today," she replied.

"Very well. I'll be there in fifteen minutes."

"You're coming here?" My father's employees feared my presence in the office. That could be explained by Tulio Bellini's awful mood after our arguments.

"Helga?"

"Yes?"

"Please don't call me *doctor* or *sir*, okay? See you soon."

I hung up and headed for the stairs, since the elevators in the Baronesa de Arary were the slowest way to get from point A to point B.

3

SPHINX. *Female monster to whom was attributed the head of a woman, the chest, paws, and tail of a lion, and the wings of a bird of prey. The Sphinx is primarily associated with the legend of Oedipus and the Thebes cycle. This monster was sent against Thebes by Hera to punish the city for the crime of Laius, who had taken the son of Pelops, Chrysippus, in a forbidden love. It settled atop a mountain situated to the west of Thebes, near the city. From there, it devastated the region by devouring the human beings who came within its grasp. It presented travelers with riddles; if they were unable to solve them, the Sphinx killed them. Only Oedipus succeeded in answering the riddle. In desperation, the monster committed suicide by throwing itself off a cliff. It was also said that Oedipus pierced it with his lance (see Oedipus).*

It was difficult there in Tulio Bellini's office to concentrate on the text and find the clues among the words.

It was as if a multitude of ghosts were spying on me in the midst of those thick books on criminal law. Romulo, my father, my ex-wife—all of them made their presence known one way or another. And Dona Helga, herself a member of the living dead in flesh and blood, suspicious, kept coming into the office on the pretext of consulting some paper or other. Pure simulation. Helga, unlike my father, was a lousy actress. I couldn't refrain from a sadistic impulse to ask her: "Helga, have you ever heard of the riddles of the Sphinx of Thebes?"

"What's that, doctor?"

"Helga, don't call me *doctor*. I'm not a lawyer, I'm a de-tec-tive." I pronounced the syllables one at a time, aware of the unsettling effect the word had on the office personnel.

"Yes . . . Remo . . . I don't know any riddle, no sir . . . I mean . . . Remo . . ."

"Okay, Helga, you can go now."

I admit I was kind of rude to the old lady, but I was unable to control the juvenile rebellion that overcame me whenever I set foot in that place. After all, Tulio Bellini's office was enemy territory.

Getting back to the task at hand, I followed the instructions of Pierre Grimal, who had ended his explanation of the Sphinx with "see *Oedipus*." I turned several pages until I found the *Oedipus* entry on page 127.

OEDIPUS. *Oedipus returned from Delphi, where the god had predicted he would kill his father and marry his mother. Frightened and believing himself to be the son of Polybus, he decided to voluntarily go into exile; he therefore went to Thebes, and en route encountered Laius, who began to insult him (or, according to others, whom he insulted), provoking his anger.*

Upon arriving in Thebes, Oedipus faced the Sphinx, a hybrid monster of lion and woman, who posed riddles to travelers and devoured those who failed to answer. It usually asked: "Which being walks now on two feet, now on three, now on four, and, contrary to what is normal, is weakest when using the greatest number of feet?"

There was also another riddle: "There are two sisters: one begets the other and the second is begotten by the first."

The answer to the first riddle is "man," because he crawls in infancy, then walks on two feet, and leans on a cane in his final years.

The solution to the second riddle is "day and night" (the noun day is feminine in Greek; therefore day is "sister" to the night).

No one among the Thebans had ever succeeded in solving these riddles, and the Sphinx had devoured the candidates one by one. Oedipus saw the answers immediately, and the enraged monster hurled itself from the top of the cliff where it lived (or Oedipus pushed it into the abyss).

4

When I arrived at the office at six o'clock, I found in the waiting room, beside Rita's desk, a doctor (or orderly or something like that) and two armed police officers. In Dora's inner office, in addition to her, were Boris and the scribe, sitting around her desk. Across from them, seated on the sofa, were Sofia Rafidjian and her son Samuel Rafidjian III—Samuca—who was providing support. Boris was the first to speak, checking his watch.

"I hope you have a good reason for all this theater, Dora Lobo. I've already said my time is precious and that I have to be back at the precinct in half an hour."

She simply smiled and lit a Tiparillo, then rose and went to the window, where she stood motionless, staring at us as would a teacher before handing out a tough exam to her students. "There are times when the exercise of my profession becomes difficult, unpleasant, and, above all, deeply painful," she said. "This is one of those times. First, I want to say that I don't take the slightest pride in this, and I have the obligation to reveal this information in defense of truth and the freedom of a man unjustly imprisoned."

"Stop beating around the bush, Dora," Boris prodded.

"My dear Boris, take quick action to get a court order to free Miguel Angel Sanchez Olivares. The killer of Samuel Rafidjian Jr. is . . ." At that moment, Dora dramatically extended her arm toward Sofia

and Samuca and said: "His own son, Samuel Rafidjian III!"

"A parricide . . . ?" stammered Boris.

"Ohhhhhh!" screamed Sofia, and fainted.

Samuca jumped to his feet and tried to run to the
door. The two policemen, as previously instructed
by Dora, stopped him. The doctor, or orderly (also
instructed by Dora), came into the room with a small
valise and injected a tranquilizer into a vein in Sofia's
arm to stop her from thrashing about hysterically.

Dora, who despite her efforts was unable to disguise her pride, turned to Boris and said: "Now do
you understand the reason for all this drama?"

"No, I don't understand a thing," he replied.
"Please explain."

As the doctor and Rita made Sofia comfortable
on the waiting room sofa, Samuel sat on the sofa
hitherto occupied by his mother, and the policemen
stayed outside. Dora, standing before the window,
stared at Samuel, who remained cool and collected,
if not perplexed.

Finally, she said: "It all began with a small suspicion, a subtle inspiration. The image of Rafidjian
dead with both eyes perforated reminded me, I don't
know why, of the myth of Oedipus. Oedipus, as everyone knows, killed his own father and later blinded
himself as self-inflicted punishment for his terrible

crime. The fact of the murderer having used an umbrella as a weapon, if we consider the umbrella as symbolic of protection and safety, also suggested to me the idea of aggression against the father figure. But up to there you could argue that I'm stepping into the realm of supposition and, worse, using armchair psychology to support apparently absurd hypotheses. Quite correct. But a piece of evidence confirmed my suspicion."

"What evidence?" asked Boris. "For the love of God, Dora."

"Talking to Ismalia, the family's maid, I discovered that since the day of his father's death, Samuca, displaying an unusual level of paranoia, has insisted on preparing his own meals and washing his own clothes. That seemed very odd. I could accept that perhaps he was afraid of poisoning, although we must admit that any such threat seemed very outlandish. But washing his own clothes? Why? To what purpose?

"I asked Ismalia what pieces of clothing he washed on the day of the crime, and she confirmed it was a pair of jeans, shorts, a T-shirt, socks, and a sports jacket. When I asked her if she had noticed anything unusual, she told me there was reddish water left in the basin—but that none of the clothes were red.

"That, gentlemen, is what led me to the certainty that Samuca killed his father—the red tinting the water in the sink wasn't from any dye but the blood of Rafidjian himself that stained Samuca's clothes."

"And why would a son kill his own father?" asked Boris.

"Because Samuca discovered his father was gay and couldn't accept this." She turned to the young man. "Am I wrong, Samuca?"

He maintained his silence.

"Did you know your father was gay, Samuel?" Dora pressed.

He nodded.

"Then tell us everything and take a weight off your conscience," suggested Boris in a manner both paternal and free of irony.

"How is Mom?" Samuca asked.

"Everything's all right with her," I replied, and dashed to the cabinet in search of whiskey.

5

Samuca spoke: "It began some time back, two months ago, I think. Me and two friends, Ferrer and Svanovicz, decided to go out one night in Svanovicz's father's car. First we stopped for drinks at a bar on Avenida Angélica. We had beer with Steinheger. Then we went out to raise some hell. First we harassed the drag queens along Avenida República do Líbano. I remember we stopped the car and asked one of them how much he charged for a trick. The guy said, 'I don't do threesomes.' We swore at him and got out of there fast, burning rubber. Svanovicz is a great driver."

"Do you want something to drink, Samuel?" asked Dora.

He shook his head and continued: "Then we went to the Dante Alighieri School to mess with the fags there. We were drunk and just wanted to cause trouble . . ."

"Go on," ordered Boris.

"Okay, so we circled around the block in the car yelling at the guys strutting for the johns driving by . . . We were drunk, you understand, it's not like we thought that was a cool thing to do."

"We understand," I said, just to join the conversation.

"You can keep talking, Samuca. You're among friends," added Dora, trying to mask her irritation and impatience.

"Suddenly," he went on, "I saw something that shocked me. In front of us, one of the cars circulating was a metallic-blue Monza. I knew that car. I looked at the license plate . . . QX 1492. It was my father's car.

Behind the wheel, an unmistakable silhouette . . . It was my father!"

Silence fell, broken only by the sound of the typewriter keys. After a few seconds, Samuel resumed his narration: "My father was there, going after one of those faggots. I quickly realized this but didn't say anything to my friends. Instead I said, 'Let's get out of here, I've had enough,' but at the time I wanted to scream and cry. I wanted to die from shame."

Samuca began sobbing, and Dora told me to get some Kleenex from Rita.

When I returned, Samuca had settled down, but his eyes were red and swollen. "Ever since that day, I began living with that terrible secret. I wanted to believe it was nothing but a horrible coincidence, wanted to lie to myself that maybe my father was passing by Dante by chance; but deep down I knew I was wrong."

Samuca pulled two tissues from the box on the desk, blew his nose, and Dora stubbed out a Tiparillo. Her expression indicated she was pulsing with happiness.

"Despite seeing my father in the car," Samuca said, "I needed more proof that he actually was a homosexual, so I started keeping an eye on him the nights he was home. When he wasn't, I would ask Mom where he was, and she'd usually insist he was visiting a patient. I would run to my room, where I had an extension phone, and call the hospital: 'Is Dr. Rafidjian there?' and the operators would say, 'He just left,' or, 'He hasn't come in yet.' I was getting suspicious, but didn't yet have concrete proof . . ."

6

"One Sunday night my father and I were watching television in the living room when the telephone rang. We have two phone lines: one for general use by the family, the other with a number Papa only used for calls from patients. You know what a pediatric surgeon's life is like—the phone rings all day long. So Papa kept that line exclusively for his professional use. It had two extensions, one in the living room and one in my parents' bedroom. When my father's phone would ring, he would answer it himself. That was what happened.

"'Hello?' he said. 'Yes. Just a moment, I'm going to take this in the bedroom.'

"He put the phone on the table and said, 'Samuca, hang this up when I answer,' and went into the bedroom. I knew this was my chance. Mom and Silvia were making a cake in the kitchen. Serginho was asleep. Ismalia was in her room. Nobody was in the living room, just me. I picked up the phone and waited for Papa to get on the extension. He said:

'Samuca, you can hang up now.' I answered, 'Okay,' and punched a key on the telephone like I was hanging up but kept my hand over the mouthpiece. And I heard his voice saying, 'Miguel, is that you?' The other voice, a man with a Spanish accent, said: 'It's me all right, Samuel.'

"'Thank God, thank God! Where were you?'

"'Samuel, I need dough.'

"'But didn't you get married? Didn't you marry that dancer? I've been looking for you everywhere . . . I can't stand being away from you.'

"'I did get married, but I'm broke. Can you lend me some dough? Listen, if you don't get me some, I'll tell everybody you're—"

"'Don't threaten me, Miguel!' my father snapped. 'And I've told you not to call me at home, someone might get suspicious.'

"'Sorry, it's just that I'm desperate.'

"'Meet me tomorrow at the office, the usual time, between noon and one o'clock. We'll talk then.'

"They hung up. That's how I knew the time and place they were going to meet. The next day, I decided to get there a bit early to have a talk with my father and catch him by surprise."

7

Samuca had gone to the office to intercept his father before Miguel Angel arrived. He said he didn't remember exactly how everything happened, but when he told his father, "I know you're a fairy," Rafidjian struck him with a violent blow to the face. Overcome with fury, he punched his father back and then banged his head repeatedly against the desk. "I went crazy," Samuca explained, and when he saw the umbrella leaning against the wall, he grabbed it and slashed Rafidjian's face, poking out his eyes. "I don't know why."

Certain facts would surely be considered at Samuca's future trial. For example: the coat he wore (he later washed the pants because they were stained with blood), the hood he used when he entered and left the building, confirming premeditation in avoiding being recognized by some friend or colleague of his father's (he left dressed in shorts, the blood-stained pants hidden in his backpack).

Further: right after committing the crime, he went to a luncheonette, where he ate a regular meal, and later played basketball at the Pinheiros Club, which proved sangfroid and suggested the intent to establish an alibi.

Samuca was arrested immediately, taken away by Boris and the policemen, but with a good lawyer (maybe I'd suggest Tulio Bellini to him, why not?) he'd allege temporary insanity brought on by powerful emotion and perhaps he wouldn't spend much time behind bars.

Sofia Rafidjian remained in a state of shock for several days, and even now I don't know how much repentance she feels at having hired Dora Lobo to solve the crime.

Dora, though excited, appeared profoundly exhausted after Boris, Samuca, Sofia, the doctor, and the policemen left.

"Happy birthday, Bellini." She held out a package that had been sitting on her desk, then poured two glasses of whiskey and plopped into the armchair. "Here's your present."

It was a new appointment book.

"Did my hints about the Sphinx's riddles help at all?" she asked.

"I think so," I answered. "I arrived here suspecting Samuca of the murder, but I still have a lingering doubt."

"What is it?"

"In your opinion, Dora, Samuca replicated the actions of Oedipus, right?"

"Right."

"But by killing Rafidjian, was Samuca killing his own father, Laius, or the Sphinx of Thebes, who proposed the life-or-death riddle?"

"Beats me," she said. "Ask a psychiatrist."

Some whiskeys and several Tiparillos later, I raised the question: "What do we do now?"

"We take a vacation. I'm going to spend a few days in Buenos Aires."

I returned to the Baronesa de Arary.

Later, Beatriz showed up with a present of her own. A tape with Muddy Waters and Buddy Guy playing together. The sense of mission accomplished lifted my spirits. I played the tape, and to the intoxicating sound of blues I asked: "Beatriz, did I ever tell you about Khalid?"

"Who's Khalid?"

"A friend who taught me that women are an illusion. At first I thought it was nonsense, but after Ana Cíntia, Camila, Dinéia, Fatima, and you, not to mention my ex-wife, Dora, and my mother, I believe, and even understand, what he meant."

"A guy who says that sounds like a parrot. It's just an old male chauvinist cliché. Don't buy it."

"No," I said, "you're the one being prejudiced. I learned a lesson with Khalid—that it's possible to learn something from any situation. Didn't you ever read Fernando Pessoa? 'Everything is worthwhile, if the soul is not small.'"

"Yes, I've read it. I just don't understand Khalid's lesson."

"I don't know how to look at women. That's the lesson. I live in a desert full of mirages. The problem, Beatriz, is that when it comes to women, I'm as myopic as Boris with those huge glasses of his. I think it's time to face Zé Maria. Can you finally give me his number?"

Afterward, Beatriz and I emptied a nearly full bottle of Jack Daniel's, to the sound of Muddy Waters, Buddy Guy, and, inevitably, Robert Johnson. In the wee hours of the morning, as she was getting ready to go, she announced she was leaving for Europe in two days.

I couldn't accept that on the night of my birthday, and on the eve of her departure on a long voyage, Beatriz still wouldn't agree to spend the full night with me. My mood immediately soured.

"Have a good trip," I said.

"What?"

"I said have a good trip."

"Are you mad at me?" she asked.

"Of course."

"Why, Remo?"

"For countless reasons. The first, obviously, is because you don't want to have a serious relationship. Fine. You don't want to, you can't, and there's nothing I can do about it. But it also seems like you're not even interested in being my friend, and you don't make the slightest effort to develop our relationship beyond sex. All you demand of me is fleeting pleasure in bed, but I need a more stable relationship. It must be something about your upbringing . . ."

Beatriz said nothing. For the first time, she didn't rebut my arguments with evasions or psychobabble. Her body and spirit seemed to be possessed by a terrible morbidity.

Then I realized what I'd done: "Beatriz, forgive my insensitivity! How could I not see it earlier?"

She seemed to emerge from her trance and looked at me questioningly. "Not see what?"

8

"That you were raped as a child!"

A thundering guffaw shook her entire body. Amid her uncontrollable laughter, she managed to say: "Remo, stop being crazy. First you think I'm a lesbian. Then, that I'm married. Now you think I was raped in childhood. When are you going to get it through your head that you can't be a detective fourteen hours a day? Relax. Stop trying to discover my problem."

"It's just that *your* problem has become *my* problem. And it's more complex than a problem. It's a mystery. An enigma."

"Do you think you have what it takes to solve two riddles on the same day?" she asked.

I didn't answer.

After a prolonged silence, another question: "Do you really want to know about everything?"

"Of course," I said. "I need to know."

I filled the glasses with what was left of the Jack Daniel's. We toasted. I saw that Beatriz was trembling.

After a nervous swallow, she said: "I love my father."

The blues disappeared into the air and the phrase echoed in the sudden silence in my apartment.

Some love their father. Others hate their father. Some even kill their father, I thought, trying to convince myself that all of this was normal.

Beatriz said: "I love my father, I'm in love with him. As a woman."

She could have kept talking for the rest of the night and I would still never have found the proper words to respond to that revelation.

Wednesday

I woke up (alone) with a hangover of Homeric proportions.

Livia Bellini, with her penchant for seeing religious meaning in everything, would say the hangover, at the age of thirty-three, signified a crucifixion. I, more than a crucified Christ, felt at that moment more like a chained Prometheus (the sensation was in fact that of a shredded liver).

The previous night was still reverberating in my mind. I remembered that after her surprising disclosure, Beatriz had asked me, "Are you shocked?"

Silence served as my answer.

"I think the dimensions of my soul are limited, Beatriz," I said a little while later, thinking about Fernando Pessoa.

"Want to fuck?" she asked.

It was difficult to say no at a moment when she seemed so fragile. Yet fucking was the last thing I wanted to do that night. What intrigued me most was seeing the resignation with which Beatriz accepted that unusual passion.

"What hope do you have of happiness if you're in love with your father?" I asked.

"We're happy. We accept our love. Except it hurts. Hurts a lot."

I could imagine. Or maybe I'd never be able to. I let her disappear without resisting. Then I lay down and tried to sleep, though I was confused and intoxicated. Incoherent dreams invaded my few hours of sleep.

The mystery was solved, the riddle deciphered. And I had a horrible taste in my mouth.

That same afternoon I began my psychoanalysis with Zé Maria. He advised me to reestablish relations with Tulio Bellini.

"Since it's necessary to commit a parricide," he concluded, "and in your case that parricide is urgent and inevitable." Seeing that I was looking at him curiously, Zé Maria quickly added, "I'm referring to a symbolic parricide, obviously."

I smiled, relieved (and, after all, wasn't everything a question of symbols?).

That same afternoon I gave up on psychoanalysis.

JUNE 7

Thursday

Beatriz left for Europe, promising to send me a postcard from Rome.

The night was cold, a cold that only comes in June in São Paulo.

Fatima had vanished. I thought about looking for her but didn't have the strength to get out of bed. Not that night.

The absence of Dora, who was in Buenos Aires, left me as insecure as an abandoned infant.

Howlin' Wolf on the tape player. *"I'm sittin' on top of the world . . ."*

I heard the sound of two cars colliding on Avenida Paulista, but I wasn't sure if I was dreaming.

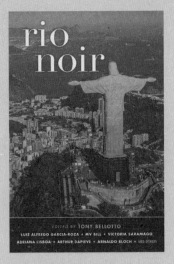